# CLOUD 8

# CLOUD 8

## Grant Bailie

PUBLISHING

*New York*

# Cloud 8

Published in the United States of America by
Ig Publishing
Brooklyn, New York
*www.igpub.com*

*10 9 8 7 6 5 4 3 2 1*

ISBN 0-9703125-2-0

*To My Parents*

# -1-

When I died (car accident, other driver's fault), there was a long black tunnel at the end of which, bathed in a pure white light, stood Abraham Lincoln. I was as surprised by this as I had been by the other driver, and when I stepped out of the end of the tunnel into the patently glorious light I asked him: why you? Why not my mother or someone else I had known?

During my life I had been neither politically nor patriotically inclined, so Lincoln—or any president—seemed to me an odd choice of greeter.

"I'm not Abraham Lincoln," said the tall man with the thin, deeply lined face, the long, bent nose, the wart, the beard and the stovepipe hat.

"But the hat, the beard, even the wart . . ."

He made a face that deepened its lines but meant nothing and handed me two pieces of paper. One I recognized as a baggage claim ticket; the other was a small scrap with an address and some other numbers scrawled along the bottom in a handwriting that looked suspiciously like my own.

"A lot of people dress like this here. I wouldn't make too much of it," he said.

I found this hard to believe, but it turned out to be true. When I went to luggage claim—and found that I had one suitcase—about half of the sky caps looked like Lincoln (except for the hat), and the driver of the cab waiting outside also bore an uncanny likeness to the 16th president. He drove me to the address on the paper and when I got out, the man exiting the building that I was entering looked like Abraham Lincoln as well.

The building turned out to be a post office, or something that was enough like a post office that it was pointless to call it anything else. It had bright white lights and a worn brown tile floor. A winding line contained by red velvet ropes led to a white and gray Formica counter. The vague, dusty smell of mail hung in the air.

Two bored-looking clerks behind the counter processed whoever was next in line, reminding the rest to step back behind a yellow stripe on the floor.

I studied the people in line, looking for some sign of their respective endings—a knife in the back, a hole in the head, a noose around the neck—but it seemed as if they had all died of boredom, tedium, or neglect. And why should I be surprised? I myself did not have a steering wheel imbedded in my chest or a dashboard knob where my right eye should be.

Opposite the counter and its slow-moving line was a wall of a hundred or so small, numbered brass doors. I figured that the number at the bottom of the paper could have been a box number, so I checked the wall and, finding my number, reached (instinctively?) into my pocket. In it was a key. I opened the box, found an envelope inside, opened the envelope and found another piece of paper and, taped to it, another key. The paper had an address—this time neatly typed—and I sighed at what seemed to me a ridiculous waste of effort. I went outside and caught another cab.

"Why not just give me the second piece of paper first?" I asked the cab driver, who, I found myself relieved to see, bore no resemblance to any historical figure beyond a slight and passing one to Mussolini. "What do you mean?" he asked in that disinterested tone people sometimes use when they are stuck in a car with you and it is impractical for them to be anywhere else.

"I mean, why give me one address just so I can go and pick up another address? Why not just give me the address I needed first? I mean, as long as they're handing out addresses, right? For that matter, why give me a key to open a box to get a key? Why not give me the second key first as well? As long as they're handing out keys."

"You in a hurry?"

"No. Not that I know of."

"All right then."

"OK."

I sat back and looked out the window at the buildings going by.

I seemed to be in a city. It seemed to be night. Buildings glittered, ending in points or blunt squares against a black, full-mooned sky. The streets and sidewalks were wet, as if it had just stopped raining. A few clouds that could have once held water slid weightlessly over the surprised face of the moon.

On the sidewalks there were men and women of varying age and appearance, some walking together romantically as couples, some walking and laughing in large groups, and some walking stoically alone. The buildings they walked in front of seemed to be stores and businesses. Everything appeared to be well-lit and carefully maintained, but none of it eerily so, which is to say, none of it divinely so. I could see, here and there, a scrap of paper, a leaf-clogged sewer, a weed growing between cracks in cement, and it seemed likely that, if I could have looked closer, I would have found a cigarette butt or two squashed against the sidewalk.

# CLOUD 8

It could have been any mid-sized city, really, except for the circumstances of my arrival and the preponderance of people who looked like a certain well-respected and long-dead president.

"How far is this place?" I asked the driver.

"You in a hurry?" It seemed to be a favorite question of his.

"Just curious."

"Not far."

We pulled up in front of a building: a five-story brownstone lit by two yellow spotlights hidden among the shrubs in front. The spotlights made thick, black shadows out of the thin lines between the stones and the occasional dark shape of a leaf, stirred by some faint breeze, fluttered ghost-like across the building's face. It was a face made slightly moronic by the wide-set window eyes on the top floor, and by the tall, undecorated facade above, that shone in the moonlit night like a bald, bland forehead. The front door, painted red, stood open—an idiot's mouth—at the top of three cement steps.

"Here you go," the driver said.

"Thanks. Do I pay you?"

I patted my pockets—for show mostly. I didn't expect to find anything else.

"Did you pay the last driver?"

"I don't think so. But I was still a little disoriented back then. I was in a car accident and . . ."

"Then you don't pay me either."

"OK. Well, thanks, then."

I got out of the cab and watched it pull away. I studied the license plate as it shrunk into the night: black numbers on a white background with no mention of county, state or country. I don't know what I was hoping for. Some clear sign from God or the universe, coming to me in the form of a vanity license plate—would it read 2-RTH or B-U-TEE? 4-SAK-N or RE-DEEMD? G-SUS? But it was only numbers. If I was the mathematical sort maybe I could have made sense of that—maybe I could have found some part of one simple equation that explains all the mysteries of the universe or tells the one true name of God. But I was not the mathematical sort and only recognized what may have been part of a phone number I once had a long time ago.

I went up the steps and entered a lobby that seemed familiar to me, but not so familiar that I had the impression I had been there before. If anything, it was an amalgamation of every apartment building lobby I had ever known: lobbies where the smell of soap and varnish are part of a tangible atmosphere lit by the golden glow of flower-shaped glass lights hanging from walls on curling brass stems. A red carpet led from the foyer to the staircase, and two small still lifes—a bowl of fruit and a vase of flowers—hung in simple wooden frames on the beige walls above a well-worn leather couch.

I carried my one suitcase to the fourth floor (the number on the key was 402), found the door, unlocked it and went in.

A man was there, frozen halfway between standing and sitting on the couch behind him, obviously startled by my sudden appearance. With some struggle against the forces of momentum and gravity he straightened himself and said, "Well hello there!" And then, his balance completely restored, he turned and repeated: "Hello there."

"I'm sorry," I said. "I thought this was my apartment. The key . . ."

"It is," he said. "Our apartment, at any rate."

I looked at him. He was a man about my age (34 at time of death) and of a generally pleasant, or at least nondescript, appearance. A little pale perhaps, but not deathly so. His face was lean, bland, smiling, looking a little like the building itself. His hair was receding across his broad, shining forehead. I wondered briefly if it would continue to recede in this place or if its progress had stopped at the moment of his death (and I assumed instantly that he was a dead man, like myself; there was nothing about him that had the air of angel or archangel).

He held out a hand for me to shake and said:

"I'm Scott." And I said: "Hello, I'm James."
He nodded. "Well, hello there James."
"We're roommates then?" I asked.
"Yes. Roommates."
I tried not to seem disappointed.
"Do I have my own room?" I asked, my expectations of the afterlife having been sufficiently lowered by now.

"Oh yes. Certainly. It's not as bad as all that. I'll show you it. I imagine you're anxious to see what's in your suitcase, huh?"

"Uh-huh."

"I know I was." His smile broadened to show off-color teeth and the pink edges of his gums.

"Yeah. Seeing how I don't remember packing one before I left," I said, but in fact, I had more or less forgotten about the suitcase in my hand.

"This way," Scott said, leading me down a small, narrow hallway. My bedroom was the second door of two on the left. The other doors in the hallway—as Scott pointed out with the cheerfulness of a real estate agent—were a closet, his room and, at the end of the hall, the bathroom.

My room had a small bed, an empty bookshelf, a dresser and a closet. There was one window that overlooked the tops of two trees. The bed had a simple black headboard with three pink flowers painted on it. The walls were neutral-colored and bare. The size and shape of the room reminded me in some way of a child's bedroom—perhaps even my own bedroom as a child.

I put my suitcase down on the bed while Scott stood in the doorway smiling in some way that may have been intended as sympathetic.

"Who knew heaven was a furnished apartment?" I said, popping open the latches of the suitcase.

"Don't think of it as heaven," Scott said.

"That shouldn't be hard."

"I'll let you settle in. I'm going out in a few minutes but I'll be back tonight if you want to talk or anything."

"Thanks."

"There's beer in the fridge."

"Thanks."

"Help yourself."

"Thanks."

He closed the door quietly as he backed out of the room. I opened the suitcase. Inside, packed as carefully and efficiently as a box of chocolates, were my favorite sweater, my favorite shirt, my favorite pajamas, my favorite pair of pants, my favorite socks and underwear, my favorite book, my favorite record, my favorite coffee mug, and the Daffy Duck glass that I had loved and broken as a child.

I took out the glass, looked at it for a moment and almost wept. It seemed the perfect symbol of everything I once had and had now lost. Life for example, or love, or youth. I took it to the kitchen and filled it with beer.

I drank three beers from my long-lost glass while poking around the apartment. I opened cupboards, drawers, medicine cabinets and closet doors to see what sort of odds and ends this pseudo-heaven contained. They were the odds and ends all apartments contain: coats and coat hangers, shoes, dishes, towels and sheets, toothpaste and toothbrushes, razors and cream, soap and shampoo, dead batteries and dust. The apartment itself was like most of the apartments I had had during my life. The walls were all beige with one or two mysterious stains. The floors were hardwood, uneven, scarred and darkened by several decades of re-coated varnish. The faint ghost of greasy, inept cooking hung in the air.

In Scott's room (I peeked discreetly from the doorway) there was a bed, dresser, a pair of shoes and nothing else.

I refilled my glass, sat down on the couch and turned on the TV.

There was a funeral scene on. However, it was a sunny day instead of a dramatic gray and rainy one, as usually used for death scenes. For a moment I imagined the film crew, having stood around for too long waiting for the weather to become more suitably overcast, finally giving up and going ahead with the show.

Folding chairs had been set up in the grass around a casket that was already being lowered by mechanical pulleys into a neatly dug hole in the ground. People sat in the chairs, their hands folded on their laps or covering their mouths as they coughed politely and the priest finished off his generic words of comfort. All of it had the flatness and uninspired direction of a soap opera and at first I thought that maybe that was indeed what I was watching. But it was something else.

These were not soap opera actors, but people I knew. Friends and family. I tried to imagine what circumstances surrounding my death could have warranted such news coverage. Was my job more important than I imagined? Was the other driver a celebrity, politician, or leader of industry? But there were no captions, no hushed commentary of newsmen, no whispered summary of events from an off-screen man in a suit conversing with the on-screen man and woman in the studio ("Is it true, Dan, that Mr. Broadhurst left behind many loved ones who dearly miss his presence now?" "Yes, Cheryl and Mike. In fact if you look at the front row you will see his father, clearly moved by the events, and next to him . . .").

On the screen, my father was sitting in the front row. He was crying—softly, the way my father cries. He held my wife's hand tightly in his. She looked sadly (but without tears) at the pile of flowers on the casket. Susan, my sister, was at my father's other side, her hand resting on his arm. Next to her was her husband, and next to him my oldest brother William, his wife Maggie, and my other brother Thomas.

I looked carefully at the rest of the crowd and found that they were all friends, neighbors, co-workers, aunts, uncles, cousins, and the friends of cousins. A good crowd of dutifully and respectfully unhappy-looking people.

The casket descended. The little wheels creaked (oh the strain of my dead body; my earthly shell; it was several pounds overweight at time of death). I tried to imagine myself being lowered into the deep hole, tried to see my funeral from the dramatic angle of the box descending, but on TV it remained a static shot from slightly above, showing the mourners, the priest, and the coffin lowering into the shadows, past the neatly cut edges of artificial grass.

The Priest solemnly intoned "from dust to dust" etc., and I whispered "Amen" with my lips against the rim of my Daffy Duck glass and began to weep quietly.

The coffin hit bottom with a quiet thud, and two men stepped forward to unfasten the cables that still held the casket to its contraptions.

Clicking the remote several times quickly (just to see), I found that my funeral was playing on every station, as if I had been royalty, a president, or a star of stage and screen.

Eventually the crowd began to disperse. People left the scene in little, respectful clusters, stopping on their way to shake my father's hand or hug my wife or nod sadly at my brothers and sister with looks meant to speak volumes of unspeakable sympathy.

Scott came home.

"It's my funeral," I told him. "It's playing on every station."

He smiled and said: "Very nice. Very nice. It's not good to watch too much television, you know."

"Every station is me," I said. It occurred to me then that I was perhaps more than a little drunk. I straightened myself on the couch and set my half-empty glass down on the coffee table with a precision intended to show that I was otherwise.

"Thanks for the beer," I told him. "That's my wife."

"Very pretty."

"Thank you."

Grant Bailie

My father, wife, sister and brother-in-law were getting into a car.  My two brothers lagged behind in the grass, talking quietly to each other, their voices too soft to hear above the starting of engines.  They laughed about something—perhaps some warm memory of me that they were sharing.  We had all three shared a quiet, rueful, respectful and ironic laugh at my mother's funeral about how she had once thought you could get cancer from burnt marshmallows, or from sitting directly in front of the TV.  She had died of cancer when I was eighteen, but it was an unmarshmallow-related black spot on her back that killed her, contaminating her flesh and spreading, via the usual biological highways and byways, to her brain.

A line of cars wound their way slowly through the cemetery, past trees and tombstones, past a mausoleum, past a group of mourners just arriving—the next show—and out onto the busy streets.  Purple flags waved from all the antennae, faces somber beneath windshields that showed the sliding reflections of treetops and clouds.

"It was a beautiful funeral," I told my new roommate.  "My father cried.  Very nice sermon."

Scott went to the kitchen, brought back a can of beer, and sat down on the couch next to me.  I picked up my glass and showed it to him.

"I broke this when I was a kid," I said.  "I

bought it from the store with my own money. There was a sale and I'd wanted one real bad, so I bought it with my own money. But I had to carry it in a bag while riding my bike home from the store. I made it all the way home but it was raining a little and the bag got wet and ripped just when I got to the end of the driveway and the glass fell out and broke."

"I had a blanket when I was a kid," Scott said. "I took it everywhere with me, but then lost it on vacation when I was five. It's in the hall closet right now. Isn't that something?" He sighed and added meaninglessly: "You never know."

"I cried when I broke this glass," and tears were welling up in my eyes as I said it. "My Dad made me go sweep the pieces up off the driveway while I was still crying. But now I have it back."

On TV the cemetery was now empty of all but the workers who had stayed behind to fold the chairs, fill in the hole and take away all the specialized equipment.

I put the glass down on the coffee table, got up unsteadily and said: "I think I'll go to bed now. Show's over, I guess. TV's all yours. Thanks for the beer."

"Don't mention it," he said.

I went to my room, put on my favorite pajamas and went to sleep.

I dreamt that I was a phantom drifting

through the walls and furniture of my office at the last company I worked for. The desks were empty; it may have been a holiday. Then I was flying over the scene where my life had ended. All that was left now was a dark stain on the pavement (blood? motor oil?). I circled once or twice, like a vulture, then moved on, over green fields, past high-tension wires and billboards and the autumn red leaves of trees that did not even stir as I passed through.

I flew home. Home to the charming, white bungalow (so said the real-estate ad) where my wife sat smoking a cigarette in front of the TV. Dear pretty wife, with her smooth black hair, white skin, long neck and red lips. So prettily they sucked at a long, thin cigarette. A woman's cigarette. So sadly she exhaled a mournful cloud of blue-gray smoke.

We had bought the house two years before my untimely and tragic death. It once had a flower garden in the backyard, but neither my wife nor I were even amateur gardeners, and within three or four seasons it fell into a state of casual ruin.

There were happy memories in that house, and this seemed like the time that I should be thinking of them. But as I hovered there in front of my wife, still in her funeral clothes, I saw only the dent I placed in the wall once during a fight, the water stain in the corner of the ceiling from the time I let the bath overflow, and the spot beneath the window sill where the paint had dripped down (I was always inept with a paintbrush, particularly around trim).

She sipped from a glass of wine, leaving the red print of her lips on the rim of the glass. The filter of her cigarette was also stained red. She smiled at something on the TV and smoke leaked out from between her teeth and from the two perfect commas of her nostrils.

I left the house through the back wall, flew out over the yard, over the garden whose once-sharp edges were now dulled by weeds and grass, out over rooftops of my former neighbors, across highways and the small, young forests that grew beside them.

I hung a graceful left above freshly plowed farmland and flew across the small town that led to my father's house. There was the corner drugstore where I had bought my comic books, and later, condoms, there was the field where we played baseball, the street where we played kickball (ghost runner on first, ghost runner on second, ghost runner on third).

I entered through an open window, though I knew I easily could have gone through any wall. It was the house I had grown up in, an old, white, Victorian house with broken and missing gingerbread in the eves, and upper-floor windows that had always seemed, in my youth, like intelligent and watchful eyes. The front porch was a distended, grayish jaw with spindly teeth.

My father was in his living room, sitting on the couch, watching TV. It was a different show than the one my wife had been watching. A cheetah stalking a young zebra through tall yellow grass. There was a tear in my father's eye. I wanted to sit next to him. I wanted to watch his show with him and tell him that I loved him. I wanted to tell him that my Daffy Duck glass was whole again and that all had been forgiven.

# -2-

I awoke the next morning to the smell of coffee brewing and eggs frying (and maybe burning a little around the thin white edges) reaching out to me from the kitchen like the vaporous hand in a cartoon. I spent little time wondering if all of it—the Lincolns, the city, the post office box, the cab rides, the apartment, my funeral on television—had been a dream. I got out of bed, put on my favorite pants, shirt, and sweater, took my favorite coffee mug out of my suitcase and went into the kitchen.

"Good morning," I said to Scott, who was standing by the sink in a robe and pajamas. "You made breakfast."

"Um . . . no," he said. "But help yourself."

He smiled apologetically and added: "I made coffee."

I saw then that the frying pan was in the sink and there was only one plate—with two eggs and a piece of toast on it—set at the table. He had made coffee though. I washed out the frying pan, put it back on the stove and got some eggs from the fridge.

"It's not exactly what I thought it would be," I said while the eggs were cooking and Scott was finishing off his own breakfast.

"Breakfast?"

"This afterlife thing."

"No. I guess not."

"Breakfast too, for that matter, but the afterlife in general I mean."

"I can imagine."

"How long have you been here?"

He shrugged. "It's hard to say. A little while. A while, I guess." He seemed to think about it some more, adding up the figures in his head while he chewed, before coming up with his more exact and final answer: "Quite a while."

"You like it?"

"Not exactly what I thought it would be, either."

I poured us both a cup of coffee, put cream and sugar in mine, asked him what he wanted in his and found that he took it black. I sat at the table across from him, sipping my coffee while the eggs finished cooking. He chewed his food carefully and wiped his lips with the back of his hand every 30 seconds or so.

"I would like to ask you some questions about all this," I said.

Looking up from his empty plate he said:

"Mm. Yes. But I have to get ready for work." He wiped his mouth again, took a last sip of coffee. "Maybe when I get back . . ."

"Sure."

"OK?"

"OK."

He took his coffee with him to his room. I ate my breakfast while he dressed and was washing the dishes when he said goodbye.

Later, with my third cup of coffee, I sat down on the couch and turned on the TV.

In the same flat soap opera style of my funeral was an interior shot. Kitchen. Day. My wife wore the green silk robe I had gotten her for our last Christmas together. She was putting dishes into the dishwasher. She finished loading, added the soap, closed the door, and turned on the machine. She sang to herself as she walked from one room to another, picking up stray things and putting them in their place. The song was unfamiliar to me, and not overly familiar to her either, it seemed. She sang the words in an unsure mumble. Now and then the robe slipped open a bit and I saw the soft, shadowy line between her two (should I say ample?) breasts. Sometimes a stray, curling black hair fell across her face, and she brushed it aside with the back of her hand or a puff of her breath.

On another channel my father was raking

leaves. The leaves, still wet with dew, clumped together under his rake. Poor frail aging father. Cloth and flesh and muscles sagging from his bones, he reminded me of a poorly made tent. Everything was falling and slipping away except for his cheekbones, which were like hard, red balls beneath his wet eyes. He raked and bagged, then tied the bags.

He had not been an emotional man for most of his life; I had never even seen him cry until the day he told me that my mother had cancer. But from that time on he cried easily—weeping indiscriminately at funerals, weddings, movies, TV shows, and commercials for long distance phone service or old-fashioned lemonade. At such moments, he often looked up at the ceiling or the sky to keep the tears from spilling out over the red rims of his eyes. Sometimes he said disparaging or distancing things to whatever it was that was having this effect on him. To a commercial he would say: "Sad-sacky," or "Silly." To a movie: "Good acting." I seldom saw him wipe his eyes, or the tears running down, though all the same, it was crying. At least a kind of crying. Somehow, though, he managed to suck the wetness back in through force of will, or the aid of gravity.

I changed the channel. In an empty office, my brother William sat at his desk.

On yet another channel Susan fed her baby,

and on another Thomas prepared to wash his car, which was white and bleeding rust from various scars and holes on its body.

My old office was there on TV as well. An empty cubicle in an empty room of cubicles. The papers and artifacts (a picture of my wife, a red and blue scribble drawing by my nephew) had been cleared from my desk and wall, and a cleaning person I could remember nodding to politely in the evenings was putting a new plastic liner in the empty wastepaper basket. I vaguely recalled the project I had been working on before my death: an advertisement for a hair cream that had long gone out of fashion. "Restore that 'just shampooed' luster" was a phrase I had been working over in my head for days without satisfaction. "It's not your father's hair cream" was another. Mercifully, I had been killed before the deadline.

Flipping through stations quickly, I saw scenes of other people I knew doing those dull, menial or serene things that seem to filter down through the days of the week and collect themselves into a small pile at the week's end: going for walks, shopping, trimming hedges, cleaning the house, etc. They were my family, friends, neighbors, coworkers. They were the populace of my past life, going on with their lives as I would have imagined them to. But none of it was quite so tender or heartbreaking as my own funeral. After an hour or so I turned off the TV and went outside for a walk.

It was sunny. A few clouds spread themselves out in thin white strands across a blue sky. No birds sang. No dogs howled mournfully. No golden shafts of light descended dramatically from the sky, but the vehicles that went by in the street— red, yellow or blue taxis and buses—were shiny and well-waxed, unblemished by rust or dirt, possessing inside their perfect shells smoothly-oiled engines that did not grind, mufflers that did not rattle, and exhaust pipes that did not belch smoke rancid with the stink of burning oil.

I walked a long way, past houses, trees, apartment buildings and downtown glass office towers. I must have walked miles, and at a nice steady pace, but I did not feel tired. What I felt was something like that illusion of inexhaustible energy and fresh promise that rides so softly on the air of the first spring day, but it did not fade with the change of a breeze, nor wash off with a few drops of rain. The sun shone and on and on I went, without feeling lost, without getting tired, wondering if this, at long last, was the benefit of heaven.

# -3-

The day I died—the second before I died, even—I was driving back from my sister's house, having spent a pleasant afternoon there chatting over coffee and playing with her son. My nephew was a sweet-natured, towhead, cherubic boy named Robert. He was not called Rob or Bob or Bobby—his mother and father were nearly tyrannical on this point—but Robert, after our father.

I had left my sister's house humming. As I drove, a song that I liked was playing on the car radio. I had a full tank of gas, which always made me feel better about myself and my place in the world.

Before entering that fateful and fatal crossing I was casually reviewing the day's quiet events.

I had come to my sister's house to deliver a toy to little Robert, a toy that was exactly like one I had owned myself as a child. I had been thrilled to find it a few days earlier in a store near where I worked. The toy was a circular, metal drum, painted with the happy, nose-less, large-eyed children one often sees painted into the blank spaces of toys, with two red wheels on each side of the drum and a long plastic stick handle. When it was pushed across the floor small bells inside the drum tumbled and hit against other things and a music that did not seem nearly as random as it should have was created. That music was the wordless song of my happy, uneventful childhood.

My nephew was temporarily overjoyed at the gift, as he was by any new object, but he returned a few minutes later to the one-armed action figure he had been playing with before my arrival.

"He loves it," Susan assured me. "He'll love it."

"Do you remember?" I asked her. "We had one just like it."

"Except it had a wooden handle," she said.

"Did it?"

"Of course."

"What of course? It was exactly like this one. The handle. Everything. It has the same pictures on it even."

"They didn't have plastic back then," she said.

"They did. Of course they did," I told her. "It was the age of plastic."

"Well maybe they had it, but they didn't use it much." But I knew I was right and she was wrong. I could easily recall the many brightly-colored plastic objects of our youth: buckets, blocks, cars, trucks, Frisbees, Wiffle Balls, hollow plastic bats with wood-grain patterns molded into the surface. I'd had a box of plastic Civil War soldiers, half of them gray, half of them blue. And Susan herself had owned an all-plastic tricycle, whose large, hollow front wheel had been worn down into flat angles.

"I think ours had monkeys on it," she added.

We fell silent for a moment and watched little Robert play. He was saying over and over again what my sister informed me was his newest and most favorite word.

"Kablam," he said, swinging the action figure's one arm in a wild punch at the air.

"Kablam," he said, dropping the figure onto the carpet and stomping on it with his foot.

"Kablam," he said, throwing it blindly into the air, then panicking when the figure landed behind him somewhere out of sight.

"It's right behind you, Robert," my sister told him, and I laughed as he tried to turn his head, but was limited by his infant lack of neck.

Not long afterwards I left, got into my car, drove the familiar streets back toward the house where my wife and dinner were waiting, heard a song I liked on the radio, pulled into an intersection less than a block away, and promptly lost my life.

Do you want to know about the squealing tires, the breach of traffic law, the blood and dying that followed? Or the fact that I was not wearing a seat belt? What thoughts flowed through my brain as the blood they traveled on became less and less? Does dying, violence, the sound of breaking glass, and first aid interest you? It does not interest me. Not anymore. If death meant nothing more than a different city and the ability to walk tirelessly, it at least cleared my mind of thoughts about the gruesome end I came to and how I could have prevented it. I simply died, went through the tunnel, met my first faux Abe Lincoln and collected my luggage.

And in that new life, how quickly I fell into an old routine: coffee in the morning, beer at night, walks on pleasant days, TV, and sometimes weeping at the dull sadness, happiness, and general unfolding of lives. My father, sister, brothers, nephew, wife, friends and former coworkers went on and on. The world that spun in some other section of space, time or dimension spun without me.

Scott came and left with his usual hellos and see-you-laters and let's-talk-sometimes. But we did not ever seem to talk and as time passed it seemed less and less likely that we would—that I would ever sit down with him and ask: So what is this place

and how long am I here for? What are its bound-
aries and what is my contribution toward rent and
groceries?

He was, in some ways, the perfect roommate. He did not ask questions or bring home dates.
He was neat, even-tempered and quiet. He was not
stingy with the beer—but where was my Virgil to
escort me through this land beyond? Who would
explain the best bus routes or show me the sad, pin-
ing faces and fates of my lost loves?

I walked the sidewalks of the afterlife alone,
looked at the people I passed without knowing who
they were or how they had died, looked at the pretty
girls with the same vague longings I had looked at
them with when I was alive. These buildings, trees,
and streets became familiar too. I took comfort now
from certain neon signs, from street lamps,
Abraham Lincoln, the periodic and reliable changes
in the weather, from the quiet, polite regularity of
my roommate, and the full moon that hung brightly
in every clear night sky.

But this second world held no more answers
than the first and as time went by I no longer expected them, the same way you go through your first
life, eventually coping with your doubts of purpose,
meaning and reward.

The days that passed formed a pattern, a
rhythm. Days of sun and blue skies were followed

by days that were partly cloudy, followed by gray skies, followed by days of rain (usually light, but every fourth cycle or so heavy and slanting). And on clear nights always (always!) a full moon and a polite smattering of stars. But somehow the days only passed. They did not add up. Defying any numerical system, refusing to organize themselves into neat piles of weeks, months and years, they laid themselves out calmly in a row that faded off into the distance at both ends.

Scott slipped in and out of the apartment with his own rhythm and pattern. Scott—no last name. Off every morning to a mysterious job that he never acted mysterious about. Yet he never spoke of it and effortlessly brushed off whatever questions I might have. He was so good at it that, after he had gone and I was left alone with my cup of coffee and my morning shows (my wife dressing, my father shaving, William kissing his wife goodbye, Susan feeding little Robert breakfast, etc.), I would not immediately realize that he had evaded me again. How many days in a row had he done that? Weeks, if they existed. I couldn't count them, but it seemed absurd that there was always some happenstance to rush him out the door: a bus he suddenly had to catch, a thing he had forgotten to do.

One day I asked him: "What do you do at work? For that matter, how is it that you even have a job? What kind of place makes a dead man work?"

How could he escape that? He was not standing by the door. He could not leap out of the window; it would have drawn attention to himself.

"Have you checked your mailbox lately?" he said, putting on his coat.

"Hmm?" was all I could think to answer.

"You should check your mail." He was heading for the door now—escaping, I knew, but I only sipped my coffee and thought about my post office box as he slipped out again.

I walked that day (partly cloudy; tomorrow it would rain) with a new sense of purpose: I was going to the post office. I was going to check my mail.

My pace was faster, my mind focused—not on the trees, sky, buildings or pretty girls around me, but on where I was going, on the quickest way there and the distance that remained. I could have taken a cab, I suppose, or even run there, but I had grown fond of walking tirelessly on the unbroken sidewalks of the afterlife. A steady rhythm built itself into my thoughts when I walked; it wrote wordless songs that seemed capable of being number one hits in any world or dimension. I remembered when I had been alive, hearing people talk about something called a runner's high—some euphoric sense of well-being and strength that came only after pushing through the pain and exhaustion of exercise. It was the glorious reward athletes received for breaking through the metaphorical wall of one's own body. Perhaps this was something like that, but I remembered also that that metaphorical wall and the euphoria on the other side of it had something to do with certain chemicals being released in the brain—and did I still have those chemicals, or even a brain? Certainly I seemed corporeal enough, and appeared to be walking in a real world of houses, trees and taxicabs, but how reliable was all that evidence? The food one eats in a dream has the taste of real food; the women one loves are soft and breathing, but when you wake the sad residue that is left behind is only yourself. Your stomach growls because you have not really eaten anything at all.

But there was the post office in front of me— its bricks as red, it corners as sharp, its roped-in lines as real as any I had known back in my former life. I went inside, pulled the key from my pocket, opened my little brass door and found that I had mail. One envelope, addressed to me, a stamp in the corner with a portrait of Lincoln. No number on the stamp.

I did not open the letter there. I have never been one of those people, dead or alive, who could open mail at the mailbox in front of mailmen or whoever might be passing by. (I picture a sunny, country scene for such people. Smiles on their fresh air- faces. Ruddy cheeks. White teeth. Green grass and blue skies behind them. Nothing to hide or be ashamed of. What have you got there? asks a neighbor. Letter from my son, daughter, wife or husband; let me read it to you without checking first if it is at all sordid or sad or personal.)

I would always take my mail inside, place it on a table, prepare myself in one way or another— a cup of coffee, a can of beer, a glass of wine—and then sit down. When I was ready, I would push the bottom edges of all the envelopes flush with each other, shuffle the deck, as it were, and then open the least interesting one first. Inevitably it was something like an announcement that I had won a million dollars or a cruise to Barbados, or that I was eligible for a new gold, platinum, titanium or uranium credit card.

I placed my one letter in my jacket pocket and headed for home. It began to rain. Had I lost track or had the pattern changed? It was a gentle rain as usual, and a warm rain, as always. I did not mind the feel of it on my face, or the weight of each drop slowly adding itself to my clothes.

At home, I hung my wet jacket by the door, placed the envelope on the kitchen table, poured a beer into my Daffy Duck glass, and sat down. I took two sips, then opened the envelope.

Inside was one page, typed.  It read:

*Dear Mr. Broadhurst:*

*We are pleased to inform you that you have been accepted for a position at the Komacor Corporation.  As Vice President of Human Resources, I look forward to meeting with you soon to introduce you to the Komacor Corporation family and to discuss your place in the company with you.*

*I have taken the liberty of scheduling your orientation meeting for tomorrow morning. I trust this will be acceptable to you.*

*Best of luck in your exciting new career path.*

*Sincerely,*

*Bob Lenworth*
*Vice President of Human Resources*
*The Komacor Corporation*

There was no date or address, but I felt certain that any cab driver could take me to the

Komacor Building directly and that "tomorrow" meant the day that followed today. I refolded the letter and returned it to its envelope. I took my glass of beer and headed for the couch.

On channel 1: my wife in her office, talking on a headset phone.

"Well, Mr. Hauser," she was saying. "I'm sure you would like to pay this off now before it's reflected in your credit history."

A pause. She examined the points of her fingernails, and turned the page of a magazine on her desk, filling in the O's at the top of one page with a pen.

"Wouldn't you, Mr. Hauser? Yes . . . Yes . . . But don't you want to take care of this *now*, Mr. Hauser? Don't you think that would be in everybody's best interest, Mr. Hauser? "

Again she stopped to listen, to let Mr. Hauser speak for a bit in his own defense, her lips stretching naturally into a broad (should I say predatory?) smile. I could see a red smear of lipstick against the white of her front teeth.

"I think it would, Mr. Hauser. I think it would be in *everyone's* best interest to take care of this now, Mr. Hauser."

She took a cigarette out of her purse and tapped its end lightly against the desktop. She pressed a couple of buttons on her computer, placed the cigarette in her mouth, then took it out again.

"That's not what our records show, Mr. Hauser."

One beer, two beers, three . . . in my Daffy Duck glass.

I drank steadily throughout the day, until the effects of the alcohol took possession of my body and my mind. I am usually a pleasant enough drunk; liquor can make me talkative, sentimental, philosophical, or sleepy, but only rarely does it make me surly. The night I dented the wall in the family room is an example of this less desirable effect (a night I would rather not talk about). And this night, while I squandered a nameless day drinking in front of the TV, watching my wife fondle an unlit ciga-rette and perform the evil duties of her job, I felt another of these moods descending upon me, coat-ing everything like a fine dust that dulls the surface of whatever minor beauty the world might contain— the sparkle of chrome, the gleam of plastic and glass on like-new appliances.

Eventually Scott came home, a vaguely dis-approving look on his indistinct face as he saw me sitting there, the TV chattering away in my wife's voice.

He said his customary "Hello."

I answered, not slurring my words, but spit-ting each one out cleanly: "Hello Scott. How was work, Scott? For that matter, what is work, Scott? Just what is it you do for a living, Scott? If you don't mind my asking once again, Scott."

"For a living," Scott laughed. "That's funny." His laugh was a small, uncertain thing, like the clearing of a throat. Clearing his throat before a lecture maybe. He hung his coat by the door.

"So what do you do, Scott?" I asked again.

"Have you been drinking all day?"

"That's right. That's what *I* do. That's *my* job, so what do *you* do? I told you mine. You tell me yours, Scott."

He glanced at the TV. My wife was on her way home from work. Stuck in traffic, she alternated between mumbling along to a song on the radio and swearing at the driver of the car in front of her. Cigarette ash fell onto her lap. She brushed it away.

"Too much TV isn't good for you," Scott said.

"Thank you, Mom. You know my Mom used to say that too? She used to say that you could get cancer from sitting directly in front of the TV, so she always sat off to the side. Made us all sit off to one side. Great big TV set in the middle of the living room and the entire family huddled into a corner looking at it from an angle. She said the same thing about microwaves, but that was my Mom.

Always sitting off to the side of things.   And you know how she died?"

"Cancer?"

"Yeah.  Yeah!" I raised my voice.  I could hear it bouncing against the walls, rolling across the floor, dripping from the ceiling.  "Did you read that in the holy phone book or something, Scott?  Did you see it on the news . . . Action Eight Afterlife News or some such fucking thing?  How did you know, Scott?"

He shrugged and looked around the room uncomfortably, like he was looking for a way out. And who could blame him?  I would not want to be in a room with me acting like that.

"It stands to reason," Scott said.  "The way that you asked the question."

"Oh.  Stands to reason.  Well, Scott, you'll be happy to know that I've got a job now too.  So all your mysterious shit isn't going to mean all that anymore.  I start work tomorrow."

"You shouldn't drink so much, Jim."

"It's James."

"James."

"I don't like Jim.  Or Jimmy.  My parents named me James. Respect that. You should respect that."   I took a sip from my glass—a careful sip so that I wouldn't dribble beer down my chin and un-dermine the wisdom of my insightful remarks.  "And

I also shouldn't watch so much TV. It's not good for me. It'll give me cancer."

"I'm going grocery shopping," Scott said. "My advice to you is to stop drinking, turn off the TV and get some sleep."

"Thanks Mom," I said. "Thanks for the un-asked-for advice."

He put his jacket back on and left. I smiled meanly at the door closing after him, then frowned. At least I hadn't punched him or the wall. I hadn't even gotten off the couch.

On TV, my wife had arrived home and was changing out of her work clothes. Off went the blouse, the skirt, the pantyhose (graceless things). I looked without passion at the smooth whiteness of her flesh, the gentle swell of her stomach, the roundness of her hips, breasts, etc. It seemed a dust had fallen over that world too. From a great distance, I tried to remember touching that body once. Once (more than once, many more times than once), I had my way and effect on it. But all that was gone now, the reality as well as my memory of it.

On went the sweatshirt, the jeans and the socks. The sweatshirt had once been mine. It had the name of the University I briefly attended on the front. The sleeves were frayed and too long and she had to roll them up to wear it. But she did wear it.

# Grant Bailie

She did.  I began to cry.

# -4-

The Komacor Corporation occupied the 42nd, 43rd and 44th floors of the second tallest building downtown. A few years back, when I had been alive, the rage had been to make skyscrapers in the style of ancient Roman temples, but elongated, simplified and translated into the modern materials of steel, cement and glass.

That style, or perhaps its architects, had preceded me here. The building in front of me (picture me looking up with the gawking awe of a tourist) was a sixty-story rectangle of black glass, framed at all four corners by massive unpainted steel columns. The columns were fluted, and ended high up in the hazy distance with all the traditional capitals and arrangements of sculpted leaves. But the columns held up nothing and the building itself continued up without them, eventually tapering off to a dull steel point poking into the sky.

Through revolving doors I entered the lobby—a vast expanse of black marble floor, rose marble walls, and brass elevator doors. Three security guards sat behind a long, curving desk at the far end. I walked toward them—and might have heard the ominous echoing clicks of my heels marking my steps across the lobby had the air not been filled already with the sound of dozen of sets of other heels clicking and shuffling their way back and forth with no sense of drama whatsoever as several elevators emptied at once. The guards did not look up from their desk as I approached. They were working on something.

"Rouge to Pierre . . ." the first guard said.

"What does it start with?" the second guard asked.

"Pickled fish," muttered the third to himself, perhaps working on a different section of the puzzle.

"What about twenty three across? What the heck is that?"

"Neither brew netting nor blonding be . . ."

"What the heck is that?"

"I have an appointment with Bob Lenworth," I told all three of them. "In Human Resources. At Komacor."

"43$^{rd}$ floor," one of them said, not bothering to look up while he pointed to the elevator bank on the other side of the lobby.

A chorus of angels did not sing as I crossed the lobby; Satan, Father Time or Jesus Christ did not wait by the door asking me "Up or down?", and I wondered why such things continued to surprise and disappoint me.

A fat man in a blue suit got into the elevator with me, rode up in silence, and got off at the 20th floor. A small, pretty woman with brown skin and yellow hair got on at the 25th floor (she smelled vaguely of some spice or flavoring I could not name) and got off at the 35th. I ascended the rest of the way alone.

On the 43rd floor, the doors opened onto a small lobby with green carpeting and large photos of happy people (satisfied customers?) on the walls. Another attractive woman—brown hair, no particular smell—sat behind a high wooden desk, smiling as I came toward her. Was she dead like me? And how had she died? Were they all dead, every face I passed on the streets or in hallways, every cab driver, bus driver, receptionist or clerk? It seemed somehow wrong to ask them, the way it is wrong to ask the person you meet on the sidewalk or in an elevator how much money they make. It is something you may ask family or roommates, perhaps, but no one stranger than that.

"I have an appointment with Mr. Lenworth. My name is James Broadhurst."

The woman directed me to an office down the hall. I knocked lightly at the door and was told by a deep voice inside to enter. It was oddly comforting to find Abraham Lincoln sitting behind the desk inside.

He stood up, gesturing me toward a chair. "Mr. Broadhurst, have a seat," he said, reaching across the desk to shake my hand. "I'm Bob Lenworth."

We sat down. I noticed that his chair, aside from being slightly higher than mine, was the old-fashioned sort you might find in the balcony of a century-old theater: dark Victorian curls of wood, red velvet upholstery, a high back. His stovepipe hat was on his desk, resting on a stack of papers.

"I've been looking forward to meeting you, Jim," Bob Lenworth said. "Looking over some of your past work here," he nodded toward the papers under his hat. "Very impressive."

"Yes?" I thought for a moment that this might finally be the point, that maybe he would pull out a large, leather-bound book with yellowed pages filled with all of my deeds and misdeeds, and tell me if the world would have been a better or worse place without me. This might finally be the permanent record so often alluded to by nuns and teachers. However, looking at the stack of papers peeking out beneath his hat, I recognized the top sheet as my résumé.

"So where do you see yourself in the

Komacor Corporation, Jim?" he asked. "If I may be blunt. Cut to the chase, and all that."

"Uh . . ." I said. "What exactly *is* the Komacor Corporation? To be perfectly honest, Mr. Lenworth . . . if *I* may be blunt . . ."

"Call me Bob. We like to think of everyone here at Komacor as family."

"Well, to be perfectly honest, Bob, I have no idea what your company does."

"Quite a few things, Jim. Quite a few things. Too many to mention, in fact. But I am certain we'll find you a position here that will make you happy. Something suited for a man of your talents."

"My talents . . ."

"Yes. Shall we talk about your talents, Jim?"

He moved his hat and picked up my résumé. It was the last one I had made—not even mystically changed to include an important project I had completed just prior to my demise.

"You've worked extensively in advertising, I see."

"Is that a sin?"

A smile worked its way into the deep, presidential lines of his face. "That's funny," he said. "I can see why you were in advertising. Clever. The Komacor Corporation could certainly use a sharp mind like yours."

"Does Komacor have an advertising depart-

45

ment?"

"No." He coughed once and placed his hat back on top of the stack. He studied the sheet in his hand for a moment, then placed it face down on the desk.

"Let me ask you a few questions, Jim. Standard stuff for these interviews."

"OK."

"Do you smoke?"

"No."

"Drugs?"

"No."

"Drink?"

"A little."

"Who doesn't, right?"

"Right. Though some people don't, of course . . ."

"Do you have a valid driver's license?"

"Well . . . That's a bit hard to say . . ."

He made a slight frown and glanced down at his desk, shifting his hat a little to look at the corner of another sheet.

"Yes," he said, nodding. "I can see how there might be some confusion on the matter . . ."

"It was valid before that."

"Of course."

"Yes."

Moving on.

"Would you say you got along well with your last employers?"

"Reasonably so.  Yes."

"And your coworkers?"

"Yes."

"Ever had any conflicts with fellow workers?  Uncomfortable situations?"

"No.  Nothing of note.  Nothing out of the ordinary."

"Are you now or have you ever been a member of the Communist Party?"

I stared at him for a moment before answering, "No."

He smiled.  "Sorry, that's my own little joke.  I like to ask that, just to lighten things up."

"I was wondering."

"Have you ever stolen from an employer?"

"No. Except some pens maybe.  Paper clips.  That sort of thing."

He nodded as if he understood and perhaps had even done it once or twice himself.

"Have you ever witnessed a coworker stealing from an employer?"

"No.  Except the pens and paper clips thing again."

"What would you say is your most valuable quality as an employee?"

"Besides my sharp mind?"

He laughed. "Yes. Besides that."

I thought about it for a second, or at least pretended to. "I like people . . . I adapt well to situations."

"That's two qualities."

"I adapt well then."

He nodded. "If you had to describe yourself in terms of the weather, what sort of day would you say you are?"

"What sort of day?"

"Yes."

"Is this one of your joke questions to lighten the mood, Bob?"

He laughed in that quiet way people do when they are watching you fail to understand something that they themselves understand perfectly well—the way you laugh at children opening a carton of milk or a monkey confused by a mirror. "It does seem silly, doesn't it? No, it's a real question. Just answer it as best you can."

"What sort of day am I?" I considered. I suppose I had been asked equally ridiculous questions before. On one job interview I had been asked to list my four favorite colors in descending order and then to give each of them a boy's name. And once my wife had given me a quiz from a magazine to determine our compatibility, asking me how I put the roll of toilet paper on the holder; did I prefer my sheets tucked in or loose; did I like Christmas more than Valentine's Day? So why should I have expected any more from this world that seemed already so much like the last one?

"A day like yesterday," I said.

"Oh? What was yesterday like?"

"Sunny and pleasant."

"So you would call yourself sunny and pleasant . . ."

"With a few clouds."

One bushy eyebrow raised itself above his eye. "I see."

"Is that the wrong answer?"

"There aren't any wrong answers, Jim. It's not that sort of test. And you've passed with flying colors. Would you like to see your office?"

"I'd love to, Bob."

~

My office was on the 42nd floor. It contained a desk, a computer, two chairs, and just enough space left over for one man to pace nervously. A window took up the whole of one wall, overlooking the city below. It was something of a promotion compared to my last office, but a distinctly minor one.

Standing at the window, I could see the streets below me moving with the primary-colored

traffic of taxis and buses. The sidewalks were writh-
ing with people. Everything glistened with the
wetness of a sudden and brief shower as sunlight
broke its way back into the sky through a thin sheet
of clouds.

Looking farther out to see where this land
stopped—to see if this world was a globe, a disk or a
square ending in epic mountains or apocalyptic
flames—I saw only a landscape that became more
green and less distinct. Buildings became smaller
and less frequent, roads narrower, trees larger, and
a milky haze seemed to roll in from some unknown
land beyond to obscure all borders and endings.

I turned from the window toward my desk,
my computer and the work that waited for me.
Proofreading, it turned out, was the job befitting a
man of my sharp mind.

# -5-

Home again, and back again to work the next day and the unknown day after that. There was no paycheck at the end of the week, but there was no definable week or weekend either, and I found I could visit any store, pull what I felt I deserved or needed from the shelf, then wait in line for a cashier who scanned and counted off each item but asked for nothing in return.

There was no rent, no cab or bus fares to pay, no fatigue from endless walks, but where were the museums in this world? The bookstores and libraries? The symphonies? The new songs of late songwriters as sung by angels? Where were the latest works by the great masters who died so long ago? They had gone, I imagined, to a *better* better place.

So every day I came and went back to the apartment I shared with a stranger, to watch my lost loved ones on TV while I drank from an endless supply of beer in a glass I had broken and cried over as a child.

Each night I slept, and dreamt every night

that I was a phantom flying over the fields, roads, homes and offices that I once knew from lower heights.

Each morning I awoke without the benefit of an alarm, but I would always get to work on time; if I dawdled or if I rushed, it made no difference. The time I got there was the time I was meant to arrive. But it was a world without time. Without the spinning hands of clocks or the pages of calendars torn off by an invisible hand. An uncountable week or month may have—must have—passed, but on TV things moved forward at a different and indecipherable rate. My nephew had walked unsteadily once, and now he strode. He had once used one word (kablam) for all occasions, and now he told his mother that he loved her and he was hungry and wanted to watch his favorite show.

Was my father aging too? Had the lines in his face deepened, his head sagged, his spine bent? William's hair was growing thin. Thomas plucked out a few gray strands from his scalp and dropped them into the bathroom sink. On TV, at least, the seasons were changing, but at a rate that was hard to follow. The grass grew and was cut with an unnatural frequency. Or it did not grow at all. The yard filled up with leaves that stayed for too long or were gone in an instant. The seasons of snow, mud, and green-then-red leaves were twisted out of order by the jerking, inconsistent passage of time.

And my wife, adapting so well to widowhood, never wearing black or crying anymore, began to date again. I drank my beer as I watched her shower, dress, and apply makeup. She tested her red lips on a piece of toilet paper and examined the mark she left behind. There was a knock on her door (once mine, too) and she answered it. A man stood before her. He was taller, stronger, darker and handsomer than I was, than I am.

They went to a restaurant (I would have only taken her to a movie) and talked about their lives. She told him about me. She told him how it was not a perfect marriage, how the romance had left long before I left the world. He was understanding, this tall, dark and handsome man. He nodded thoughtfully, and rubbed his broad, smoothly shaved chin. He understood the need for passion.

And to prove this point, at night, they undressed each other tenderly. He kissed each point of my wife's body. He slid his hand across curves, folds and openings. She responded in little breaths and gasps and moans. Did she make those same sounds for me? They seemed different now, quieter and farther away.

She returned his kisses, reciprocated his attentions, took parts of him into her mouth (I say so delicately) as he made the sad idiot face of a man in ecstasy.

I turned off the TV. Another day had passed and it was time for bed. There was work to be done in the morning.

# -6-

The Komacor Corporation (it stumbles off the tongue) liked to think of its employees as a family. It heralded this from a banner over the lunchroom, on mugs that were given out to each new employee, and in various inspirational memos tacked onto bulletin boards throughout the building.

Occasionally it spilled from the mouths of its supervisors. "We're like a family here at Komacor," they would say with varying degrees of sincerity and passion. But, at best, it was one of those dysfunctional families with siblings that do not speak to each other, a father who hides his emotions and a mother who plays favorites. If there were holidays and birthdays in this world we of the Komacor family would have gotten each other presents we could never use and did not want. And we would have smiled politely and said nothing of our disappointment.

In my department, there was one other proofreader besides myself, a manager, an assistant manager, an editor, a technical writer, and a project leader. I had been introduced to all of them on my first day by Bob Lenworth. I had shaken hands with each, had thanked each for their words of welcome and encouragement, and had promptly forgotten each of their names and faces. By the next day the other proofreader had been transferred and the project leader had gone on vacation. Several days later, the editor left under mysterious circumstances.

My project was a user's manual for a software product that the company intended to release at some distant point in the unnamed (and unnamable) future. This product would have universal applications and an ease of use that seemed impossible to specify or explain. I read all 200 pages of the manual several times over without fully understanding what it was all supposed to do, but I knew that files could have their names changed, could be combined with other files, could be divided into separate files and returned again to their original state at the touch of one or several buttons. I knew that things could be merged and dissected in endless combinations and that the product's memory for all this slicing and dicing was virtually inexhaustible. Yet none of it made any sense to me, in the same way Algebra 101 had not made sense to me, even after it was calmly and succinctly explained to me by my calm and succinct 7th grade Algebra teacher. It came close—it threatened to jell into something like understanding once or twice along the edges of my brain, but then dissolved back into ungraspable abstraction.

"You don't have to understand it," the manager, John Landsdale, told me. His office was down the hall from mine. He sat there most days from some point long before I arrived to some point long after I left, staring at his computer, pursing his thin lips in thought, narrowing his almost colorless eyes at the screen in more thought. He had thin, flat hair the same pale shade as his flesh and it seemed as if his features were composed of nothing more than shadows, as if he were a watermark that had to be held up to the sun—or a fluorescent office light—to be seen at all.

"But how can I correct it if I don't know what it's trying to say? What any of it does?"

"Do you think it's unclear then? Poorly written?"

There was an accusation in his quiet voice, perhaps even pain, and it occurred to me that he might have written the manual himself.

"No," I said. "Not per se. The grammar and spelling are in order, for the most part. And it seems well organized. It's just that I've read it over twice now and I'm still not certain just what this thing is supposed to do."

"This thing . . ."

"The product."

"We have a name for it, you know."

It was true, and that was another issue. They had a name for it. They called it Project Omega-Beta. An absurd and nonsensical title that I had trouble saying out loud without embarrassment.

"Yes. Omega-Beta. But frankly, that name doesn't make much sense to me either, Mr. Landsdale."

"Call me John," he reminded me, but not with anything like an attempt at affection or informality. It was a request that seemed as regimented and based on proper protocol as any commanding officer's insistence on "sir." He moved a paperweight shaped like the building we were in across his desk.

"John. I mean, I could understand Omega, or Beta, or Alpha-Beta, or maybe Alpha-Omega. Even Omega-Alpha."

"You've been with us for a while now, haven't you Jim? Working on Omega-Beta."

"Yes. A while. Not a long while. But for some time. I guess." And of course I had no idea how long. Maybe a month, but the sort of month that seems to take a year to pass. Or was it the sort of year that flew by like a month?

"And you're just mentioning this now?"

"I haven't been here that long.  Have I?"

"Have you spoken to Marge about your misgivings?"

"I don't know if I'd call them misgivings, exactly . . ."

"Your *questions*, then."

"No, I haven't."

"Talk to Marge," he said.  "That's what she's there for.  She's there for your questions."

"OK.  Thanks, John."

I walked down the hall to Assistant Manager Marge Boyton's office.  She wasn't there.  I went back to my own office and looked out the window for a moment.  It was the middle of the day and red, yellow, and blue traffic moved slowly through the crowded streets.

I turned back to my computer and started to read:

*Omega-Beta (replace project name with product name for final release) is the very latest in state-of-the-art business software products offered by the Komacor Corporation.  We are sure you will find it to be an indispensable tool, whatever your particular business needs.  With virtually unlimited practical applications in any field, it is certain to become a staple in the office of tomorrow. From tasks as common as merging, relocating, or simply renaming a file to some of the more esoteric chores . . .*

I deleted the first "business," replaced "staple in the office of tomorrow," with "a mainstay in the workplace of the future," and put a parenthetical question mark next to "esoteric."

I stared at it for another minute or two, then deleted the word "practical."

~

There was a common lunch area on the 33rd floor. Along one wall was an array of machines that dispensed candy bars, bags of chips, cans of soda, paper cups of coffee, egg salad sandwiches, etc. You didn't need money, of course. You just made a selection and pressed the appropriate button. Sometimes your selection got hung up and you had to try again, so you might end up with two of the same item. Sometimes the machine gave you something different than what you asked for, and you either tried again or shrugged and took what you were given. I hit a button for coffee and a button for a sandwich and everything came out as requested. I took them to a small table by the window.

Outside, the cloudless sky had become a

deeper shade of blue, the sun had moved lower against the other horizon, its yellow light thickening into honey. The light crawled visibly across the city, coating the sides of the buildings and tinting the pavement from gray to gold.

The bread of my sandwich was stale around the edges, and I distrusted the mayonnaise.

~

The assistant manager was still not in her office. I tapped on the open door of the office next to mine. Steven Roth (technical writer) looked up from his desk.

"Are you working on the Omega-Beta Project?" I asked him.

"In a manner of speaking," he said, placing a computerized seven of hearts onto a computerized eight of spades. "Why?"

He was a man about my age, but with less hair and dark, fleshy bags beneath his eyes. When he smiled his mouth revealed two unsettling rows of off-color teeth. But he never smiled.

"I'm just trying to understand it," I said, attempting to put into my face a look of camaraderie and shared suffering. It seemed the right time to try such a look. I needed some camaraderie. I wanted to share my suffering.

"What's to understand? It's just the very

61

latest in state-of-the-art software products offered by the Komacor Corporation."

"Yeah. I got that much. But what does the goddamn thing do?"

He closed his game of solitaire and began typing. He typed quickly in a font small enough to make it impossible to read from where I was standing. When he finally answered me it was as if he were reciting a poem he was in the process of writing internally while at the same time typing something else entirely. "Sorts, generates, merges, blends, bends, sends. Matches socks, finds lost car keys, repairs damaged relationships. That sort of thing. But you don't have to know how it works or what it does. You just have to make sure John and I have got all our letters facing in the right direction."

"Uh-huh." His typing increased in intensity. His periods, it struck me, were particularly forceful and I took this as a sign that the conversation was over.

I thanked him and returned to my office.

I spent the rest of the day making sure all the letters were facing in the right direction.

~

At night, lying in my bed and not sleeping, I heard voices from the apartment next door coming through the wall by my headboard. The voices did not form themselves into actual words, but remained indistinct and edgeless sounds going back and forth. It may have been a man and woman talking. One voice was higher than the other, and the other was louder, though no more distinct. They may have been arguing. Sometimes the deeper voice would increase in volume almost to the point of being understandable. Then there would be dramatic moments when no sound at all filtered through the plaster and wood of our mutual wall. I became sleepy listening to them, as if their wordless voices rising and falling were like ocean waves lulling me into slumber.

I imagined a real conversation to go along with their abstract shouts and mutters. They were discussing a dent in the wall, and how quickly the bottle of scotch in the cupboard had gone down during the last week. They were arguing about someone opening a new box of cereal before the last one had been finished. They were fighting about a woman that the man had spent too much time with at a party the night before. And above me (miles above me) footsteps walked across the ceiling, which I imagined belonged to the girl from the party. Pretty, golden-haired girl upstairs pacing while the husband lied and defended her honor to his wife.

Pretty, golden-haired girl now pouring herself a glass of wine and laying naked with her ear upon the dark wood floor. She is sobbing softly, and the glass of wine is set in front of her eyes. The print of her lips has made the glass nearly opaque at its rim.

And when I did sleep, I dreamt, as I always did, that I was flying. Flying across the fields of my former world again and then hovering over the bed of my nephew as he slept. I wondered not about the fights of couples or neighbors, but about what sort of man little Robert would grow up to be, and what sort of job he would have, and if he would be happy and have some sense of purpose in his life.

The next day, over breakfast, I said to my roommate: "Hey, guess what, Scott. I don't know what I do at work either."

# -7-

Something had come special delivery for me in the mail. It was a box wrapped in brown paper, left at my door. It had my name on it, my apartemnt number, and nothing else. I brought it in from the hallway, poured myself a beer and opened it.

Inside the box, carefully packed in wadded paper and Styrofoam peanuts, was something I had not seen since I was a child. It was a night-light of sorts—a heavy, bulky object a little smaller than a toaster, an ornately decorated brass box with a 4x9 sheet of glass set within it like the small screen of a TV. Framing the glass was a brass relief of a couple—nearly black from time and touch. The woman stood wearing a long dress that ballooned out at the hips. She held a closed parasol over her shoulder. The man wore a coat with long tails, a top hat held in one hand resting on his hip. With the other hand he pointed off into the illusionary distance in front of them—which was the glass screen—on which was printed a hand-colored photograph of Niagara Falls. Brass trees and hills swelled around it, the branches reaching and meeting overhead to form the frame.

Inside the box was a light bulb surrounded by an acetate cylinder printed with black and white swirls. If plugged in, the heat from the bulb would

make the cylinder spin, the moving pattern projecting itself onto the glass to make it look like water
was falling.

It had been a wedding present to my parents, and when I was young I would often ask my
mother to put it in my room so I could fall asleep
watching its illusion. I remembered vividly the light
sliding across my bedsheets, the bookshelf, and the
framed picture of a blue-eyed Christ on the wall.
The smell of dust burning as the acetate heated recalled a fond memory intertwined forever with feelings of security: a mother's love, the sacred union
of my parents, and the usually untroubled character of my childhood dreams. Did my mother occasionally brush the soft, youthful hair of my head
with her hand while I slept? It seemed now that
she must have.

I tried to recall the moment in my life when
I had lost track of this once-cherished icon. When
was the last time I had asked my mother for its comfort? Maybe it had been packed away with the rest
of my mother's belongings when she died, but even
then, it seems, I would have seen it sometime after,
in some attic box beneath photo albums and chris-
tening gifts, or in some corner of the basement.

But it had disappeared from my life quietly
and without notice. No crash, like the glass that
fell to the driveway. No sobs as with certain toys or

books that I had lost through my own neglect. It suffered the fate of things that stay; it was forgotten.

And now it had returned to me. Too big and fragile for my suitcase, it had been delivered to my door. Delayed by who knew what delivery problems: improper address, duplicate names, lazy or psychotic mailmen, a war in heaven or hell.

I brought the night-light into my room, set it on the dresser, then went back into the living room. Scott was sitting on the couch. The TV was not on. Scott almost never watched TV.

"What was it?" he asked.

"Something my mom had when I was a kid," I told him. "I'd forgotten about it."

"It came in the mail?"

"I guess. Left by the door."

"Hmm," he said, not in a way that indicated he was thinking about it so much, but rather that he had decided not to think about it at all, and instead would just make this small "hmm" sound that meant nothing.

"You going to watch TV?"

"No."

"Mind if I do? I'd kind of like to see how my Dad's doing."

"Help yourself." He stood up.

I was going to tell him that I didn't mind if

he watched too, but it occurred to me that, in fact, I did. Especially if—while flipping through the stations to see what else was on—my wife should appear again with the man who now seemed to be her boyfriend.

He left the room. I turned on the TV and sat down on the couch.

My wife was on with the man who now seemed to be her boyfriend. I flipped through the channels until I found my father. He was sitting at his kitchen table eating porkchops and mashed potatoes. There was a frying pan in the sink. There was a bottle of beer beside his plate. Where were my brothers? Where was my sister? Why was my father always alone? But in fact, if I had still been alive, I would not have been there either.

I watched him eat.

When my father chewed, especially when he chewed meat, cords twanged beneath the flesh of his jaw, the wrinkles deepened around his mouth, and the round balls of his high cheekbones seemed to bounce. At the same time, his eyes stared straight ahead in a blank and absent stare. It was a look that used to unsettle my mother. It was not so much that he seemed to be thinking of something else, but that his mind seemed to have shut down completely, or at least in every section except the one or two necessary to continue chewing and swallowing.

"Robert, honey," my mother used to say. "You're doing it."

Sometimes it would be a full minute before my father could pull himself back from whatever dimension he had slipped into to say, "Hmm?"

"You're doing it again."

"What? Oh." He would then look down, take another bite, and try not to slip away again.

As I watched him eat on TV, I saw this look on his face. He was alone now, free to eat as he pleased. Free to stare blankly into space while he chewed.

I turned off the TV and went to bed.

In bed, in the dark, in my favorite pajamas, I went to sleep to the forgotten joy of water falling silently, and light sliding across my covers, the dresser, and the empty walls. In the distance, through wood and plaster, I heard indistinct voices again. I heard heavy footsteps and something that sounded like a bottle falling. Then I was flying above the hill I used to sled on—green now, the grass long and gone to seed—and on through the woods where I used to play.

# -8-

Nature abhors a lawn. The sharp edges of your bluegrassed one-quarter acre will be blurry again by morning. The row of bright flowers you hunch over at noon will dissolve like the scenery in a dream when your back is turned. Weeds find their way into everything in defiance of whatever sharp object or chemical you threaten them with.

I killed a yard and garden through neglect once, but even with care it is impossible to do anything else. Even the yards and gardens I passed in this world after were struggling or overgrown.

Yet my father always labored over the impossible straight lines and borders of his lawn; the memories of my childhood are scented with the smell of fresh cut grass and exhaust. Now, on TV, I watched him fight the elements of every season thrown at him in a seemingly random pattern. Snow, leaves, frost, drought. He fought with rakes, lawn mowers, leaf blowers, shovels, sprinklers and hoses. He fought on, and only now and then were my brothers or sister there to help. He grew older, then much older, much too quickly. He would die soon, I knew, with a rake, leaf blower, or snow shovel in his hand.

But he did not. He died quietly, in bed, as I hovered over him in a dream. I heard his breath catch a little, the way a record skips. His mouth opened, and a bit of foamy spittle formed in its corners. Was there a shudder or a rattle as air left his body for the last time? Not that I noticed. His eyes stayed shut. His mouth stayed open, but ceased to be of use.

The next day the funeral was broadcast on every channel. I stayed home from work to watch it.

It was much like my own: same priest, same family and friends, though the sky was gray as it should be for such scenes. A light mist of rain fell, wilting hair and spotting clothes. My wife was there with her new boyfriend (how much longer could I call him this?). My nephew was there with his mother and father. He squirmed in his suit as the priest delivered a sermon that, if not identical to the one said over me, was certainly taken from the same set of notes.

And dust to dust. The casket lowered to the sound of the little creaking wheels, and then there were hugs, handshakes and kisses, followed by the careful, somber line of cars winding their way through the trees and out of the cemetery, back into the busy world of traffic, houses, convenient stores and office towers.

After everyone had left, and the pulleys were disassembled and the chairs folded up and taken away, I watched as a small bulldozer came by to fill in the hole. Afterward, a perfectly sized carpet of sod was laid out across the fresh dirt.

On one side of my father's grave was my mother's, on the other side mine. The grass had grown over both mom and me. The unnaturally vibrant green of my father's sod made a seam between him and us.

I turned off the TV, went outside and hailed a cab.

"Take me to the airport," I told the driver, like the man in the movies who has someplace to go and something important to do when he gets there.

"What airport?" he said, scratching his head beneath his stovepipe hat.

This threw me. My resolve faded. "The closest one, I guess."

"I don't know of *any* airports."

"Well, back to wherever it was that I came from then."

"Came from? When?"

"When I got here. When I died. Look, my father just died. He's expecting me. He's waiting for me."

This last bit was partly bluff, partly theory and partly hope.

"There's no such place," the cab driver said in the exact tone I would expect had I asked him to go to the corner of two streets that did not meet.

"Are you sure?"

"Pretty sure. Yeah."

"Are you new to this job, by any chance?"

"No, I am not." He sounded hurt.

"OK." I sat for a minute thinking about it. The driver sat impatiently looking at me in his rear view mirror. I got the impression that he was wishing there were a meter he could start running.

"Take me to a bar then," I finally told him.

"With pleasure," he said.

~

There is always a bar. Wherever you go, there is always a bar.

And the bars always smell of cigarettes, spilled drinks, perfume, cologne, wood. The light is always dim, like a deep forest, but a forest that has been varnished, its floor swept and mopped (poorly) twice a week with some pine-scented solvent that still cannot rise above the cigarettes, spilled drinks, perfume, etc.

I sat drinking between two men who sat

drinking. I looked at myself in the mirror behind the bar, though I had to dodge a row of half-empty bottles to do so. I wore an ageless, expressionless, dead man's face. I did not look mournful or tearful, but then I had not cried when my mother died either, though I can remember vividly, a year or so later, passing an all-night donut shop at 4 in the morning and suddenly thinking of her, pulling to the side of the road and weeping. (But why? There was nothing in a donut shop to remind me of my mother. She did not make donuts or hold them in any particular esteem. The woman that I could see behind the counter as I drove by was young and looked nothing like my mother. But the way the shop glowed in an unearthly way, or the smell of pastry and sugar in the air, reminded me of something intangible and unnamable. I wept. It passed. I moved on.)

There were others sitting in the booths that lined one windowless wall. A blank-faced woman with blonde hair and a green dress sat at a small table in the rear. No voice anywhere rose above a confidential whisper except the bartender's, who stopped by every five minutes or so to ask cheerfully: "Another one?"

And I always answered: "Yes, please."

My father had raised me to be polite.

Daylight, which came into the bar in three

small slivers that pushed their way through a sign-cluttered front window, thinned into the blue of dusk.

The man next to me finally spoke.

"What a day what a day what a day," he said, maybe to himself.

"Tell me about it," I said.

He turned to face me. The barstool squeaked. "You want me to?"

I said: "I mean, I've had quite a day too."

"Oh. Yeah? What happened to you?"

"My father died. And I tried to pick him up at the airport but there isn't any airport."

"That is tough," he said. "About your father."

"Thanks. So what happened to you?"

"Got fired."

I stared at him as the alcoholic fog I had spent the last hour or so manufacturing was blown away as if by the sudden shockwave of an explosion.

"You can get fired?"

"Of course you can get fired. What'd you think? You couldn't get fired?"

"Well yeah, as a matter of fact. That's what I thought."

"You can get fired. I'm here to tell you. You can most definitely get fired."

"What for?"

"Number of reasons."

"I mean, what for you?"

"My boss is a jerk. Was a jerk. Still a jerk, no longer my boss."

"Uh-huh." I emptied my glass and looked for the bartender. He was bringing the girl in the green dress something with a colorful umbrella stuck in it. Her face, it seemed to me, had become considerably less blank. It was tired now. There was a darkness under her eyes and a shininess at the points of her cheeks and chin. Beneath her chin the flesh seemed slack and unnaturally white.

The bartender came back behind the bar, grabbed the appropriate bottle and refilled my drink.

"Thank you kindly, Ken," I said. His name wasn't Ken, or at least not that I knew of. The phrase was just something I picked up a long time ago when I had been young and alive.

And as suddenly as that I was feeling social and craved the companionship of my fellow man. Perhaps the thing that I had been missing most—if I had been missing anything—was human contact. TV didn't count. Dreams didn't count. Work didn't count. Scott didn't count. A stranger at a bar counted and now I wanted the world to swirl in the warm golden light of companionship, to radiate from its center that comforting glow, the way liquor stretches outward from its pillowy landing in the stomach, like a cat yawning. Talk, laughter, thoughtful looks. Jokes and shared wistful leers at the sight of pretty women.

"So how was your boss a jerk?" I asked.

"Let me count the ways," he said, but took a sip instead and did not continue.

I stuck my hand out to be shaken and said: "I'm James."

He stared at it for a second or two, then shook it.

"Tom," he said. "Pleased to meet you."

"So how did you get fired, Tom? What for, I mean."

"He said I wasn't doing my job."

"Oh."

"I was, but that's what he said."

"Uh-huh."

"Jerk."

"Sounds like it."

We had a couple more drinks. If payment had been involved in the process one of us would have paid for this round and the other the next. Instead we took turns calling out to the bartender for two refills, two more, one for me and one for my friend here. We did it in ever-increasing volume and I began to get the impression that the bartender did not like us much.

"Want to go someplace else? I'm sick of this place."

"Sure," I said.

We went someplace else. It was not much different than the other place, though the familiar Lincoln served us our drinks this time.

Tom and I got drunker and drunker. We laughed at each other's stories or nodded with sympathy, though I can remember nothing specific of what was said. The contents of the entire night play back only as a movie montage mostly devoid of actual dialogue. Neon martini glasses dance and bubble in crude animation. Actual glasses empty and refill. A succession of bartenders smile and nod and wipe their counters with a white cloth. Two men stagger down a sidewalk as dawn makes pink welts out of thin clouds. They are laughing at each other's jokes or at their own. Friends for life (for death?). One of them lies down on a front lawn wet with dew and dotted with dandelions and looks up at the sky. The other man stands unsteadily, looking up at the sky, too. One or two stars are left.

A bit of dialogue filters through:

"I wish you were my roommate, Tom. I wish I had a roommate like you." And that is all.

I went home in bright daylight while Scott was getting up. I muttered something like hello before crawling—clothes still on—into my bed to

sleep until afternoon. When I woke up I was grateful that Tom was not my roommate.

# -9-

For some time after my mother's death I imagined her in blackness. Although the blackness may have only been the void of my own imagination or belief; she could have been—could still be—anywhere, in any color. Perhaps in another city or a suburb, hidden from me for inexplicable reasons by some witness protection program of the afterlife. She could even be in that long-dead heaven of my youth, with all its white-robed, white-winged angels strumming harps, standing by golden gates, the floor beneath them obscured by the pure white smoke of a heavenly Dry Ice machine somewhere offstage.

But now I had lost that bright faith in just rewards and ethereal happy endings. I lost it long ago, not in my own death, not in my mother's death, but in her dying—her dying and the steadfast belief, held by herself and by her advisors, that it was anything else but death.

From the point of my mother's illness on, the word "goodbye" was forbidden in our household, as it was an admission of defeat. Even for a trip to the convenience store down the street, my dad insisted on "so long" as the only appropriate departing line. When hanging up the phone it was "Later," "Talk to you later," or "Take care."

Her last days were spent in a hospital room that I never had the chance to visit, though I have seen enough of such rooms to conjure a picture of that one: white or off-white walls, a window overlooking the flat, pebbled roof of a lower wing, beyond which lies a parking lot ("Where is our car?" say the visitors who have used up all their other subjects. "There it is, next to the green van . . . "), beyond that a line of small houses, and beyond that some trees. Inside the room, a beige end table, covered with an assortment of green plastic receptacles (a pitcher and cup for water, a shallow, oddly shaped bowl for urine). Doors with large, easy-to-use handles, unexplained contraptions sitting idle in the corner under translucent dust covers, and an insistently cheerful still life or landscape hanging on the wall. Beneath the picture, the hospital bed with all its mysterious accouterment. And my mom in the bed, her latest spiritual advisor clutching her withered and unresponsive hand. My dad standing bleary-eyed at the window, looking out at the trees and green vans.

"Dear God in Heaven," the priest or

preacher at my mother's bedside inevitably began, and went from there into a top forty of the divine platitudes that had defied the dust of two millennia. *Through God, all things are possible. Ask and you shall receive. You have only but to . . .* Etc etc etc. Raised Catholic, I cannot remember the exact quotes, but they were all of the same nature: you have only but to ask and believe and it's a done deal.

Though I missed the last plea made on my mother's behalf (as she, in her coma, did as well), I remember clearly enough the parade of robed or collared men. The things they said. The dull boom of their voices. The incense odor of their sweat and cologne. With much confidence they promised their miracle to her, when she could still listen, or to my father after that.

Though the doctors could find no cheery spin to put on the increasingly cloudy pictures back from the lab, the priests and preachers kept smiling bravely with the sincere and defiant belief of your average lottery customer. They waited patiently—the patience of the healthy—for the day when someone would rush into the room, breathless, a stack of charts and films spilling from their arms, and the phrase "In all my years in the medical profession . . . " falling from their mouths. Then the word "miracle" would be whispered and muttered and then shouted until it echoed up and down the white hallways. The other patients would throw their crutches onto the floor or out the window and radiantly emerge from their gauze and plaster cocoons. A golden glow would replace the greenish-white buzzing fluorescence and a choir would begin to sing.

No such day or miracle happened, of course. From the first priest who held my mom's hand in the first hospital room to the last in the last, disease took its own course, unabated by any torrent of words or holy water. The priests and preachers (even a rabbi once) delivered their words in the unequivocal form of a promise, and when that promise was so clearly not fulfilled, it seemed that each had a ready-made explanation handy for this obvious lack of results. "God works in mysterious ways," etc.

It was with those words that my faith crumbled. In the damp, minty breeze that blew from their mouths, the pure white clouds of my imagined heaven were blown away, exposing a structure more fragile than nothing.

I could believe in a negligent God, a non-participating God, a God that wound up the universe to watch it waddle off the table. That God made a kind of sense to me. It was the God that covered himself with fine print like a lawyer, the God that allowed his instruction manual to be so badly translated, and his many mouths to spout such unreliable things that troubled me. I was not quite so narrow or spiteful as to think that these various men of God did not mean what they said or meant ill by saying it. I did not believe then—or even now—that they sought to be remembered in my mother's meager will, or were paid per soul by their respective churches. I held no malice to any one religion, and cannot even remember the last one she officially belonged to (her final days were like a spiritual game of musical chairs, and it seemed that she was perpetually damp from one baptism or another). No, it was not a particular faith that I had my problem with, but the idea of faith in general. It was certainty that I grew to distrust.

~

But everyone and their brother has a story of lost faith, of a dead parent and how they got that way. I will not bore you with all the universals or particulars of my mother's story. She died like many others, with bloating, hair loss and dementia. No great TV-movie moments arose from her bedside, no scene where I confronted her or she confronted me as some teary memory or turning point came flooding back and we embraced as the orchestra section went nuts. We loved each other the way a mother and son love each other, and though it is true I did not cry at her funeral (in grief, like comedy, timing is everything), I have cried many times since.

~

I remember the time my father told me my mother was sick. It was in the car, after he had picked me up from school. He managed to say a few words (none of them clear) before his face collapsed in on itself and the words he was trying to form were mangled and torn apart by the trembling of his mouth. I had never seen him cry before. It was disturbing, as disturbing as the news which slowly came to me—that mom was sick.

I knew the root of her illness was a mole on her back. It had always been there, but in the previous year it had grown and changed colors, until it looked like the small, dark fist of some malformed baby trying to escape through her flesh. In the summer, she kept a bandage over it. (My father had been a paramedic once, and we always had a large assortment of bandages for every occasion lying around the house.) "You should see a doctor about that," my father or I or my siblings would tell her, and she would mutter something or make a face. She had a belief, which I later adopted for my own use, that naming a disease caused it to grow, that being diagnosed with this or that, instead of merely being someone with a hideously inflated freckle, would suddenly make her a victim of this or that.

Of course, she never articulated this theory. She only made a face and muttered something like: "Yeah, yeah." But I knew what she meant, or at least, I would come to know it. And wasn't she right? We finally convinced her to see the doctor, and after that the mole took over her life, demanding tests, demanding treatments, demanding specialists flown in from out of state. It weakened her, made her nauseous, made her forget who she was. She was dead less than a year later.

I had—still have in fact—the same mole on the same part of my back. It is nowhere near as big, but now and then, my doctor in the previous world would become bored with telling me to lose a few pounds. Wanting to find some other way of justifying the fact that there was a half-naked man sitting on butcher paper in front of him, he would say: "I would like you to keep an eye on that mole."

And I would think to myself, you keep an eye on it doctor, because I will not. It is the watched pot that boils over. It is the rotten apple from the tree of knowledge that dangles there, and I shall not pluck it. It is an evil baby whom I will not name, and thus it will not be born. Like mother, like son, Amen.

When my mother was bedridden, but had

not yet been exiled to a hospital, she asked me to write down her life story. Not that her life story was coming to an end, mind you—that would have been too close to a goodbye—but time and illness had allowed her to think things over, and it seemed to her now that there was something exceptional in her history that ought to be committed to paper.

So I sat at her bedside with a pad of paper and pen in hand.

"When I was a little girl," she began, but soon lost her place. Her brain was already swollen from the disease, her hair and memory gone. I tried to write down whatever thoughts seemed the most lucid or pertinent.

*When mom was a little girl,* I wrote. *A sick child,* I wrote. *Fever. Heart condition. A murmur. Would not live to see 30. Parents loved her. Granddad—mild-mannered fellow. Once wallpapered over all the plug sockets of the living room. 4-F from the army for two separate wars. Grandma had a dozen cats. For fear of drowning— never let mom learn to swim, though allowed to go on canoeing trips with dad on regular basis. Could not ride a bike, and later, could not drive a car. Sick in hospital, never finished school. Liked a boy name Horace Greenly who looked like Fred Astaire. Dad hated him and still hates Fred Astaire. Likes Gene Kelley. Before mom, dated a girl named*

## Grant Bailie

*Denise Kamone—didn't look like any movie star.*
*Mom and dad went to the beach. She only went in*
*up to her knees. Sign said: no Jews or dogs al-*
*lowed. Dad went to war. Dad's brother enlisted*
*too, though he was only 17. Other brother was al-*
*lergic to bees—one sting would kill him. Before*
*that, the depression—used old catalogues for toilet*
*paper. Saved string for unknown purposes. Be-*
*fore she was sick (fever, heart, etc.). Before that a*
*happy girl. Loved picnics. Never had a dog. Still*
*hates cats.*

I stopped writing when she repeated the
whole thing over three times and became bogged
down trying to remember the names of her mother's
cats. I brought her some tea and crackers, which
were the only things she could keep down. She
nibbled on the edges of one cracker and fell asleep
with the crumbs of it still clinging to the corners of
her mouth.

We never went back to the history of her life
again, and I put my notebook with its half-filled
page of notes into the bottom drawer of my desk
and forgot about it for years. I packed it with me
for several moves after that but somewhere along
the way it disappeared, slipping into the ever-ac-
commodating ether with the Niagara Falls lamp, my
comic book collection, my first girlie magazine, my
wedding ring, and all the other flotsam and jetsam

that had gathered around me since childhood, only to be thrown off by the spinning forces of time and life.

I wait in vain for its arrival by special delivery at my door.

For a month or so when I was twelve (when the watery light still lit my room, the comic book collection lay scattered beneath my bed, and the girlie magazines and wedding ring were not yet dreamed of), I would often awaken from nightmares not knowing who I was. The dreams themselves were plotless, abstract and nonsensical: I had the letter Z stuck in my head, my head was on backwards, or I was being crushed by a potted plant. Fear and confusion were the dominant themes, and when I opened my eyes, the room that had comforted me to sleep seemed alien and unfriendly. Though I did not know my own name, I screamed for my mother. She would place her hand on my forehead and say my name softly over and over until I was myself again and all the shapes around me had slipped back into their familiar grooves.

After a particularly bad nightmare, I was hospitalized for observation. My blood was extracted and analyzed, my head was run through various contraptions, but nothing was discovered and I was released. Soon after, the dreams stopped without explanation. I never dreamed like that again, but now and then throughout my life a moment would come to me while I was awake when suddenly everything seemed unclear or hazy, as if reality had become a sleepless dream.

This is how I could understand with painful acuity the lack of clarity my mother went through in her final weeks. She wanted me to write down her life story, but it had already left her. The precious cells that held the memory of her first kiss, first love, and first, second, third, and fourth-born had been hollowed out by scalpels and isotopes. I tried to recall the parts I had lived through. I remembered the cardboard wings she would make for my sister Susan and me from the flaps of boxes. I remembered the drawings she would make of the cartoon face of a cat in the margins of phone books or on the backs of discarded receipts. I remembered the way her face scrunched up when she opened an oven door. That she liked to read mysteries. That when she still knew what words were, we would play Scrabble, not for points, but to use up every letter in the box. That her favorite color was blue, her favorite candy marzipan, that she was allergic to shellfish, took her tea with cream and sugar, and sometimes said mysterious things like, "she is a cat's mother" and "hay is for horses."

But all of that is no more than the vague remembrances of a son desperate to pull back something more significant from the past, something flesh from thin air. I wish I could tell the story she wanted me to tell, the story of her life as *she* remembered it, the story of the river she rode on from beginning to end, from her first sensations to her last unremembered memories.

  I will do this: I will start with the river. And look: There are mom and dad, in a canoe, paddling upstream. She is not even wearing a life jacket! If she fell in she would sink like a rock, though my father, to be sure, would valiantly rescue her. Farther up the stream we go until it empties out into a large lake. There is a beach of white sand where my mother, with a slightly nervous look on her face, lets the waves lap gently at her shins. My father, in white swim trunks, throws his chest out into the sun. No Jews or dogs allowed, of course, but they know no Jews, and my mother's family only owns cats. Past the white sands, the lake becomes a stream again. The banks at either side are thick with green grass. Under a weeping willow stands Horace Greenly. Looking forlorn in a top hat and tails, he is weeping. The bouquet in his hand droops, and red and pink petals fall into the water. Behind him in the shadows and foliage is an indistinct figure in a white dress, a tear slipping from her non-movie-star eye. Farther upstream, on a green hill, a mild-mannered man and a cat-loving woman sit on a blue blanket.

Their darling little girl plays in the tall grass and wildflowers as they look on lovingly. She has rosy cheeks and golden hair and it seems that nothing for her will ever be impossible or difficult. No tragedy greater than a skinned knee will ever touch her life. Everything before her is bright and hopeful.

I could go farther back, of course; it is within my power. I could reverse time entirely, reel the whole thing back like a spool of film. Water running uphill, flowers folding in on themselves, blades of grass sucked back into the earth like loose strands of spaghetti, the sun setting in the East, rising in the West and my mother getting smaller and smaller until she is sliding up between her own mother's legs to begin, as she ended, in darkness. You can see how poetic, artistic and profound all that might have been (*What are we?* Someone once asked. *Arrows winged with fears, shot from darkness into darkness*, he answered himself).

But I will not do that now. I have brought her back with much effort and will not lose her to simple poetics. Instead, let me leave her here on this imagined green hill, with proud parents looking on, faces beaming, big plans forming. The sun shining in the corner of a cloudless blue sky. The little girl happy and laughing. A butterfly amuses her. A dragonfly surprises her, but cannot sting. The dot on her back that will one day kill her—that might have, given time, killed me—is now only a small and innocent spot of black.

# -10-

*With Omega-Beta (<u>replace project name</u> <u>for final release</u>) as your default office tool, you will be able, in only a few simple steps, to perform formerly time- consuming tasks that are an essential part of running any modern business today. Imagine the time and energy you will save with this powerful tool at your disposal! Imagine the increase in productivity! Imagine the efficiency!*

Imagine my pain. Turning away from the screen, I rubbed my eyes. If there had been a clock on the wall I would have checked it. And if it had been there it would have told me that the day was not even half over.

I left my office and went down to the lunch-room for a sandwich and a half-pint of milk from the machine.

Across the room, I saw Steven Roth sitting at a table with John Landsdale. I nodded in their direction. They nodded back, chewing in unison on something that seemed, judging by the intensity of their mouths, to be made of meat.

I finished my lunch and went back to my office, stared at the screen for another unnamed portion of the day, then went home.

As I walked, I discovered that there were birds in heaven after all. Pigeons. A crowd of them walked in front of me on the sidewalk. They parted to let me pass, a few of them raising their wings as if they might actually use them. But they didn't.

I passed a neon sign reading "Cold Beer On Tap." I went inside.

"I'd like a cold beer on tap," I said to the bartender.

"That sign gets them every time," he said.

"I used to be in advertising," I told him.

~

Static appeared on the screen as my wife drove home from the grocery store. Little flecks of white crawled like inchworms across the top and bottom of the image. There was no antenna to adjust so I lived with the static.

She was wearing my old college sweatshirt and drumming her fingers along the top of the steering wheel as she waited in traffic. Her lipstick had been worn away to a dark outline around the edges of her mouth.

"Fuck you very much!" she yelled to a car

that had just cut her off, as she leaned on the car horn. The man in the car in front of her probably turned around and made some gesture in response—they usually do—but all I could see was my wife's face as she smiled and waved at the driver.

The streets and sidewalks that slid by her were the streets that led home.

The static grew worse as she unloaded some grocery bags from the car. She was singing to herself.

"When love congeals," she sang. "It soon reveals . . . the faint aroma of performing seals . . . the double-crossing of a pair of eels . . ."

She had bought wine, bread, cheese, two steaks, a dozen eggs, some dull, sugarless breakfast cereal that was her favorite, a gallon of milk, and a carton of cigarettes.

"I wish I were in love again . . ."

She put the things that needed to be kept cold into the refrigerator and lined the others up on the counter.

"No more pain . . . I'm all sane . . ."

She ran out of words and began humming.

Snow seemed to be falling in her kitchen. A windy snow that did not accumulate but only blew and swirled horizontally across the screen. It obscured her, her groceries, her humming voice.

Two steaks, I thought. A bottle of wine, I

thought. And thou, I thought. And what thou is that? But I could not bring myself to really care.

Above me, footsteps were bounding (happily?) across the ceiling.

# -11-

The project leader came back from vacation. A new project editor was moved up from another department. A temporary worker was brought in as a second proofreader. There was a big meeting in the Komacor War Room so that we could do something that John Landsdale liked to call: "Reorienting our Team goals." He had used the phrase several times by the coffee maker and once more by the copy machine.

The War Room—which had sounded so ominous and impressive when it was first whispered to me through the open door of my office—turned out to be a windowless conference room on the 44th floor. A long rectangular table took up most of the room. The walls were adorned with charts depicting the upward progress of some obscure numbers, architectural drawings of the building, and—for no particular reason that I could discern—a color photograph of a hot air balloon. I was disappointed. It was not so much that I still held out some small hope for something otherworldly—a large scale map of heaven and hell, perhaps—but a conference room that matched the name "War Room," at least a little, would have been nice. Something besides the elongated beige and wood veneer box I found myself in.

John Landsdale stood up at one end of the table, cleared his throat, and began talking about the need to restructure the team, the need to refocus the team's goals, the need to work on team communication. He spoke with some enthusiasm, possibly even sincere, but after a while I stopped listening to what he was saying and started counting how many times he used the word "team."

It added up to more than a dozen before the game lost its appeal.

At the opposite end of the table, Marge Boyton was going over her notes, flipping through pages, underlining things, checking things off. I could not tell if she was following along with John to see if he had gotten everything or was preparing for a speech of her own, but when he finished and cleared his throat one last time in conclusion, she did not stand to take his place.

A moment or two of silence followed. I glanced around the table, trying not to catch anyone's eye. The new proofreader sat opposite me. She was pretty and female (as I am inclined to notice), with brown hair, red-brown lips and a small, attractive dent at the point of her chin.

Finally, the project leader stood up, though "stood up" seems too mild a phrase to describe the physical effect his standing had on the room. It was as if some great scaffolding was being unfolded or a banner unfurled. The room (and everyone in it) was now somehow smaller as The Great Project Leader took his place at the front of the table. He was tall and thin in a well-tailored gray suit, and I had the impression that I had seen him somewhere before, perhaps towering above me once on a movie screen. His clean-shaven face bore the vertical lines that usually deepen with age, the shadows of a long and narrow skull beneath. His nose was epic, with a bump of flesh growing against one side. His chin was strong and smooth, and this threw me off. The fleshy bump in the nose set me straight—he was a young Abe Lincoln. Lincoln without the beard, period dress or stovepipe hat, Lincoln at some time before he had been carved away by the forces of history, by moral compromise and by being shot in the head. It was a different look; I wondered if it would catch on.

"First off," the project leader said, clutching the lapels of his perfect suit with enormous, large-knuckled hands. "Let me just say it's nice to see you all again."

His voice boomed and seemed to take up

what little space left in the room that his height had not. It was low and loud and soft at once; fatherly and avuncular; friendly and godlike. Though I recall reading once that the real Lincoln had a high-pitched voice, which carried better in those pre-amplified times, this was a different Lincoln, the Lincoln of film and stage and the occasional TV commercial for hot dogs or mattresses.

"And nice to meet those of you I am seeing here for the first time," he continued. He paused to look at the new faces—mine and the proofreader's. "I've been away, of course, but I trust John and Marge have kept things running smoothly without me." He nodded to John and Marge.

"And Fritz," he smiled at the project editor. "You and I have worked together before. It's good to have you on the Omega-Beta Team."

Fritz—who looked exactly like a man named Fritz—smiled warmly up at the large face hovering over him like a saintly billboard.

It was an impressive start, but considering the impact of his presence, what he had to say was less than overwhelming: the same muddled muck of team dynamics, goals and achievements, the same meaningless words piled high like an idiot's game of blocks.

He went on for quite awhile, but like the manual for Project Omega-Beta, it added up to nothing.  He finally finished and then it was everyone else's turn to talk.  Several speeches followed about the importance of teamwork and team identity.

"We need to consider the dynamics of communication," someone said.

"I couldn't agree more," someone answered. "But we can't afford to lose sight of our end results."

"I think the dynamics would enhance our end results, in terms of product and productivity," said someone else.

"But shouldn't the enhancement dynamics be more closely linked to product clarity results?"

"Well certainly, we don't want to lose product interest, but it is important to balance that with the enhancement.  And keep the enhancement actively linked with the results."

The new proofreader stared down at her fingernails.  They were painted the same reddish brown as her lips.  A strand of the soft brown hair that she had pulled back behind her head had come loose and lay in a graceful, elongated S shape along the side of her white neck.

She looked up from her nails and caught my eye.  She smiled; the smile of attraction, mutual fate, or teamwork, I wondered?

I smiled back.

Just then, John Landsdale said: "Mr. Broadhurst has expressed to me some concerns as to the clarity of the document."

All eyes turned to me. Friendly, curious, predatory eyes.

Startled, I cleared my throat. "Well, yes, I mean . . ." I said haltingly. "At first. But I think I am getting the rhythm of the thing now." I took a breath before proceeding.

"I just needed to adjust my mindset to its particular dynamic, you see. To understand the team results."

John smiled. Young Abe Lincoln smiled. The pretty young proofreader smiled. Everyone smiled. Welcome to the team, I half-expected someone to say, but no one actually did.

The meeting ended and we all filed out of the War Room. Back to our respective offices. Back to deleting a word here, replacing a word there. Back to coffee and stale egg salad sandwiches dispensed from a machine for free. Back to gazing out at a city and pigeons and traffic and a blue sky deepening to violet.

# -12-

I usually walked home from work, but there were evenings when I wanted to see the streets, buildings, trees and people slide by smoothly. And see it from above, though only slightly, like the view of a dying God or low-flying angel. I wanted to look at the backs of strange heads and wonder what alien things rolled and clicked within their thin shells. The backs of necks, the dandruff on collars, a stray hair—they told me stories that I could not really know, but which I took ineffable pleasure in imagining. When I felt this way, I would take the bus.

A man sat in front of me once, with a nodule of gray, corrupted flesh dangling like a tiny punching bag from behind his ear. I wondered if it had killed him—if this small rebellion of tissue had turned malignant (as my mother's dark spot had) and spread through all the usual channels, from the back of the ear to the brain. A brief trip down a swift red river.

Sometimes it was the scenes outside the bus

window that gave me pause, things you did not expect to see, even in an afterlife as disappointing as
this one. A house on fire, for instance. And the
couple outside watching as all their things went up
in smoke. (The smell of it reminded me of camp-
fires, bringing back a pleasant memory of camping
with my wife, a wonderful weekend of canoeing,
fishing, two sleeping bags joined together in a tent,
laughing, and very little quarrelling.)

Once I saw a man sleeping on the sidewalk.
Another time, I saw two men fighting.

One evening, I passed a familiar sign: a neon
martini glass tilting back and forth. It was the bar
where I had met Tom. I pulled the cord and got off.

The dim light and air was the same as I remembered. The same blank-faced woman sat
blankly at a table. The same crowd and whispers.
The same bartender. Even Tom was sitting there
where I had seen him that one evening (how many
days or weeks ago?) as if he had never moved.

"Tom!" I said, entering with the boisterous
shout and walk of a bar regular that seemed fraudulent even as I performed it.

"Hey," he said. "How you doing, buddy?" I
knew then that he had forgotten my name.

I took the seat next to him and asked for
my usual.

"Get a new job yet?"

He smiled (wryly?  bitterly?) with just one side of his mouth.

"Oh yeah," he said.  "They don't leave you on the public dole for long in this town."

"Yeah?"

"Nice little cushy mindless job.  As always.  As per norm.  As par for the course."

"What do you do?"

"I design boxes."

"Really?"

"Why would I lie?  About a thing like that?"

"I didn't know boxes were designed, is all."

"Everything is designed, pal.  You think someone just starts slapping cardboard together on their own?  A factory of people somewhere just blindly folding and gluing and hoping it will all turn out right?  There's always design, always some guy at a table with a compass somewhere planning the whole thing out.  Good old design."

"What kind of boxes do you design?"

"What kind? Squarish.  Squarish boxes for storing boxes.  Boxes for the attractive display of boxes at all the big box outlets and box conventions.  There's an unending variety of use and function, really.  Running the gamut from box-like to boxy to the merely boxish."

"I see."

"Boxes."

"Uh-huh."

"Boxes of boxes."

"Been here long?"

"Who can tell?"

I drank my drink quickly and ordered another. I glanced at the blonde in the green dress sitting at the same table as last time, her face exhibiting the same blankness as last time. Or maybe it was a different blonde.

"Someone's got to do it, right?" Tom said.

"What?"

"Design boxes."

"I suppose so," I said. Tom's charm, or my nostalgic memory of it, was gone by now. He was just an annoying guy in a bar.

"So how's *your* job going, buddy? Still disgruntled or whatever it was you were before?"

"It's all right. I'm getting the hang of it, I think."

"That's good. Software, right?"

"Proofreading a software manual."

"Well, someone's got to do it, right?"

"I suppose."

"Wouldn't be software for designing boxes, by any chance, would it?"

"Not that I know of."

He finished his drink and stood up. He almost checked his watch.

"Well, I better be off for some shuteye. Boxes await me in the morning."

"Give them my regards," I told him as he put on his coat and headed out the door.

I stayed for a couple more drinks, then went home.

~

One day I did not get off at my stop, or the stop in front of the familiar bar. I stayed on the bus as unfamiliar streets and scenes unrolled before me, and the evening sky grew into another full-mooned night.

I had fallen asleep on a bus once, in that other world, to be awakened by the driver at the end of the line. It is an odd and disconcerting thing to reenter the world like that—to leave the tender clutches of whatever vibrating, bus-induced dream you were having to find that the soft-edged dream cloud that had floated above you has been replaced by the dark and scarred face of the driver.

"End of the line," he had said, because that is what they always say.

And then you step off the bus, moving from the last remnants of the bus dream into the reality of unknown streets. Wig shops, nail salons and check-cashing stores with just enough space between them for a dented garbage can and a small family of rats. Signs in windows, curling against the glass, stripped by the sun of all colors save blue, so that it is a blue woman, with big blue hair, who smiles bluely and holds up a blue hand with long, blue, artificial nails professionally attached. The corpses of insects lay beneath her, baked hollow by the noon sun now cooling in the evening shade. Billboards for menthol cigarettes and malt liquor peel from their brick wall backings, revealing ads for different menthol cigarettes and different malt liquors beneath them. The sidewalks crumble into a confusion of dirt, dust and treeless roots, then rise again in jagged slabs pushed from the earth like splinters.

I walked three blocks through that alien landscape, trying to find the bus home. Three blocks of shadows spilling out from the rotting edges of buildings, pooling into doorways, staining the already stained streets. I do not recall seeing any people, though I know they must have been there, going in and out of doors, opening and closing windows, turning up the volume on their radios and TV sets, trying to start cars. But in my memory it is like an apocalyptic ghost town, with only me and my footsteps, looking for where the number six bus picked up again heading in the right direction: home.

I wondered if the bus I was on now would take me to a similar ending. It did not. The buildings changed from primarily businesses to primarily homes, but there were no wig shops or broken sidewalks. There was a sameness to all of it, a familiarity to the neighborhoods I saw skating by. The bus came to no end of its line but only looped around. Its route, it seemed, was a full and wide circle of heaven, and soon the streets that I saw were the streets that I knew. I reached my stop, got off, and went home to my shared apartment, TV, unlimited beer, favorite things, comfortable bed and the trick of heat, kinetics and light that made it seem that torrents of bright water were falling inside a little brass box on my dresser and spilling out from its soldered seams to flood my room and my dreams.

# -13-

The light slid across walls and sheets, and the indistinct murmur of voices next door became the sound of water playing upon the rocks at the foot of the great falls. It brought a memory to me, with such vividness that it seemed less like the usual stumbles of remembrance and more like a dream that recalls and recasts an actual event, rewriting small bits of the truth, replacing incidental characters with stock actors from other dreams, but for the most part reenacting things with more faithfulness than your average TV movie.

I was at William's apartment. It was his bachelor party. A handful of his friends and I had drunk many drinks of different colors and flavors and eaten several squares of lime Jell-O laced with vodka or gin. I had smoked half a pack of cigarettes, despite the fact that I had never smoked before nor have I since.

We stumbled outside, a yellow cab came, and we were off to the city in a drunken montage of neon cocktail glasses, flashing lights, bright red and blue glowing signs that told us Liquor, Food, Girls-Girls-Girls, 24 hour film development and 1-hour dry cleaning.  It was not a very big town.

We stopped, of course, at Girls Girls Girls. A club called, of all things, The Big Pink House of Fun.

Inside a half-naked woman danced on a stage.  Around the stage sat a fixed row of stools, as if the stage was really the counter at some hedonistic diner and the dancing woman was our serving of steak and eggs with hash browns on the side.

We sat in front and looked up admiringly, ordering drinks from a comely waitress in a bikini top and G-string.  The cab driver came into the club with us and sat quietly, drinking water.  After a few minutes, he suddenly and angrily pointed out that the dancers were not completely nude and, at this bar, would never be.  It had something to do with local standards, state liquor laws and the proximity of the nearest church or elementary school.  Quite suddenly we all became dissatisfied.

"There's a place east of here," our driver said.  "Nice enough looking girls.  And you see everything."  He grinned.

"You see everything," my brother repeated, perhaps trying to understand.

"And I mean everything."  The cab driver's grin evolved into a leer, not at the woman who was now bent over before him gazing back from between her ankles, but at the memory of a better place east of here.

Mike, one of my brother's friends, perhaps more drunk than any of us, just said: "Everything."

It was not a particularly difficult concept, of course, but we had been drinking, and it took some shouting back and forth for the lot of us to be of one besotted mind again.

We headed back into the cold night, piling into the cab as the driver revved his engine three times (for speed? for heat? for luck?) and lurched the car forward to his Promised Land.

The club we entered some twenty minutes later was almost identical in appearance to the one we had left. Though perhaps a little darker and smokier, as if to signify our descent into a more inner circle of hell. Again we sat looking up at the edge of a stage. The cab driver sat next to us and ordered a coke, smiling broadly as he waited for us to realize the rightness of his knowledge. Here we would see everything. No patch of cloth would veil the mysteries and wonders, no string would break the smooth lines of flesh, and all the gates of wonder would open before us. And open they did. A succession of curvy women beginning as nurses, school girls, and teachers, ending up as naked women splayed upon the stage, receiving dollar bills between their teeth or pushed- together breasts, or in the strap of a superfluous garter.

A collection was raised between us and put into the right hands so that, between performances, a chair was placed center stage. A man in an ill-fitting tuxedo strutted out with a microphone.

"I'm told there's a young man named William here tonight," he said. "Don't be shy. Raise your hand William. Let us see the blushing groom-to-be. The doomed man."

William raised an embarrassed hand and everyone applauded, whistled or booed.

"Dead man sitting," the tuxedo said, and then went into a two minute monologue about marriage in general, my brother's marriage in particular, and the vagaries of desire.

None of what he said was particularly funny, but in the spirit (and spirits) of everything, we all laughed as if it were.

After he finished, a dancer came out wearing the usual non-outfit, though in white for the occasion, with a wedding veil thrown on top.

She waved and blew William a kiss.

"Hello," I heard him say, as if passing her in the hallway at work.

"Oh hello, William. Are you sure? Are you really sure you know what you're doing? Marriage is a big step."

"Reasonably sure," he muttered.

She climbed from the stage and sat in his lap.

"Reasonably sure, huh?  What a shame. What a waste."

"Reasonably reasonably . . ."

She laughed again, a big head-thrown-back forties-movie-star laugh, and ran her hands through his hair.

She pulled his head into her chest and I thought I heard him mutter, "Well true love and all that," but it was hard to tell in the noise of the place, with his words muffled as they were.

"Come on," she said, getting to her feet and taking him by the hand.  "I have a little show for you. Just you."

She led him onto the stage and made him sit in the chair, cuffing his hands behind him.

We all laughed and laughed as she danced around him, taking off what little there was for her to take off, draping her white garters, her white bra, her white panties around my poor brother's head and shoulders.  She put the wedding veil upon his head as we all laughed and hooted and called out his name.

She then sat on his lap again, grinding herself against him.  She cradled his face within her impressive breasts and threw back her head again in what was now her trademark laugh. She draped her long legs over his shoulders and wrapped them around his neck as she arched backwards to the floor.

It was funny, though perhaps not ha-ha funny, because, along with everything else, our bachelor did not know where to look. Having all this before him, there was still an inborn sense of politeness in him. He did not want to stare rudely and directly. It was like that with me as well. Even drunk, even hooting with the others like a crude idiot, I looked hardest at the women when I was looking at them in a mirror, in the reflection on the ceiling above, or in the mirrored wall behind them, where it seemed unlikely they would catch my gaze or interpret my desire.

Eventually the guest of honor was released from his torment and allowed to stagger back to his seat. He tripped on his way off the stage but we caught him, slapping him on the back, saying rude or congratulatory things and expressing our insincere envy for what he had just been through.

The night passed. The women danced. The drinks were expensive and, in our cheapness, we sobered some. One or two of the dancers began to stand out in their beauty and one in particular, I thought, had the face and body of an angel. I looked at her and studied her and worshipped her in my quiet, sipping, ice-chewing way. I was still drunk enough to make a larger thing of it, to see God, beauty and the order of the universe within the gentle swell of her stomach, the opening of her thighs, and her nearly anachronistic ability to twirl two tassels in two directions at once.

One of my brother's friends tapped me on the shoulder and pointed out another woman he thought the nicest, but she was too thin for me, and there was a glazed look on her face. She opened and closed her hips without emotion. I looked at her and felt sad. I looked at the one I liked and thought I saw pleasure in her face, and I felt that she enjoyed dancing for us this way, and that once or twice she perhaps even looked my way with meaning and tenderness as she tucked away another dollar bill.

Our funds became low and it was decided that we should go somewhere where we could afford to stay drunk, rather than face the sad, painful arrival of our inevitable hangovers before the sun. No beautiful dancer, no amount of nudity seemed worth that fate.

"There's a good bar I know," the cab driver said. "South of here. No dancers, but cheap booze. A real nice place." We cheered him. He was our saint and mentor that night. We thanked and praised him profusely. He laughed at us.

We waved goodbye to the dancers. We actually waved.

"Goodbye!" Mike shouted, like a little boy leaving home for the first time. Mike off to school, bidding farewell to his stripper moms: "Bye-bye! Goodbye!"

The cab took us south, out of our city, and into one of the surrounding towns.

I looked out the window at the things gliding by and slowly began to realize that all this was familiar to me. The streets that we passed were the streets that the school buses of my youth had traveled. There was the corner store. The supermarket. The library. The school. We drove by the hospital where I was born.

"I grew up here," I said to Mike, who was crammed next to me in the backseat. He grunted and smiled in response. This place meant nothing to him.

I looked back at the hospital as it retreated into the night and fog of the rear window—an ugly red brick monolith swallowed up by blackness.

"From shirt sleeves to shirt sleeves," I muttered, which meant nothing applicable and no one, fortunately, asked me to explain it.

We arrived at the bar the driver had spoken of so fondly. The Easy Inn, the sign said in shaky, hand-painted letters. The driver led us through the front door.  There was no cover charge.

Inside, men and woman clamored for drinks at a square island bar.  Small tables cluttered the floor, booths lined the walls and two pool tables filled an adjoining room.  I could hear the clicking of pool balls and the dull rumbling of the bowling alley next door.  We ordered drinks and found that here we could still afford the pleasant numbness we had grown so fond of.  Even the cab driver indulged in a single beer.

We sat at a wobbly table in the corner and watched as a steady flow of people walked by.  We looked at the women and wondered what they would look like dancing naked on the table in front of us. It seemed that our hearts, having been weaned that night in the strip bars of the city, couldn't quite fathom this new land where certain curves and openings were kept hidden from us.

This being the town where I had been born and raised, I began to wonder if I would see anyone I had known in my youth.  I tried to think of whom I would even want to see again.  I had not enjoyed much in my fearful younger days.  But there was a girl I'd had a crush on in high school—a beautiful girl whom I remembered, perhaps inaccurately, as a Botticellian Venus.  But did I want to see her here, in a bar in this same small town?  Did I want all her hopes and dreams (she talked sometimes, I remem-

ber, of a life in New York and the theater) to have
been beaten down to nothing more than this?

But I was here, and perhaps she could be
here as well with as good a reason as mine—hauled
along with drunken friends by a knowledgeable cab
driver in search of economical oblivion. Perhaps I
could see her again, and we could talk, and I could
somehow kiss those unkissed red lips I was remembering with so much sentiment and so little accu-
racy.

I looked through the crowd. Women were
whispering into the ears of men. Men were whispering into the ears of women. They all nodded and
laughed. The people at my table shouted.

I never saw her. Her name was Pamela
Bennett and I would never see her again. Not in
that life.

"This is my hometown," I told the cab driver
as he drove us away, back to the city of my eventual
death some years later. "I was born here."

"That's what hometown means," he said.

I nodded. I was in no condition to argue
with his sober, irrefutable logic, though, for some
reason, I could not quite believe that it was true.

~

The memory played itself out to its anticli-
mactic and real-life end (work in the morning, nau-

sea, thirst, an argument with my girlfriend—my future wife, my future widow). My vision, such as it was, became just pieces of scenes lacking a cohesive structure. There was more from which to make a story, of course. William's wedding three days later would have made an appropriate finale. Instead the images dissipated, and I could see only the empty blackness of my room, like the blackness of a movie theater after the reel has completely unwound, the lights have gone out, and there is nothing more to show.

As I lay there in the darkness, the voices of my neighbors became momentarily clear, as if the sound, winding its way through the spaces between the walls like a rat, had found an opening into my bedroom.

"It isn't what you said," the woman said.

"Then what is it?" the man said.

"Not what you said . . ."

"The way you said it? Is that what you're going to say? The way I said it? Because if I have to hear *that* tired old line one more fucking time . . ."

"If it applies . . ."

The voices receded, back into the wood and plaster, back through winding and narrow passageways, over pipes, under wires.

Above me the footsteps returned, and I

imagined them this time as the feet of a beautiful stripper as she made her exaggerated walk across the floor.

I fell asleep and did not dream about any of it, as I might have if I had been alive, but instead flew once more over the streets, fields, yards and homes of my past life. Over my father and mother's graves, my sister's kitchen table, my nephew's bed, my wife's house, the homes of my brothers.

# -14-

When I awoke the next morning, Scott had already left. I made myself breakfast and caught the bus to work.

The three guards sat at their marble desk working on their usual crossword puzzle, struggling this time with a three-letter word for a former head of state. I thought maybe I knew the answer (was it Les?) but I did not stop to help. I nodded hello and continued on to the elevator where the usual mix of pretty, handsome or nondescript people accompanied me up. I got off at my floor, said hello to my various coworkers on the way to my office, sat down, turned on the computer and looked out the window. People, cabs and buses churned away as always below. Another day, I thought, and once could have added "another dollar."

First a cup of coffee from the communal coffeepot in the hallway, then sleeves rolled up, hands and brain plunging into work. I deleted a word. I replaced a word. I rearranged two chapters and renamed another. I combined two chapters into one, but then thought better of it and split them up again.

There was a knock on the door.

"Come in," I said, and the pretty new proofreader entered. Pretty brown hair down around her shoulders. Pretty brown eyes. Pretty red-brown lips. Pretty white skin and dimpled chin. Pretty.

"Hi," she said. "I don't think we've officially met. I'm Mary."

"Mary," I said, wondering for a moment if I should rise from my chair, but having taken time to wonder, the time for doing so had passed. I remained sitting but held my hand out across the desk.

"I'm James."

Her hand was warm, small and soft.

"Can I ask a stupid question?" she asked.

"You can try."

"What does Omega-Beta do exactly?"

"Sorts, generates, merges, blends. Matches socks, finds lost car keys, alleviates headache pain, whitens whites and brightens brights."

"Oh."

"I can't figure it out either. I just make sure all the letters are facing in the right direction."

"I see," she said and smiled. Attractive smile. White teeth, the foremost one of which was endearingly crooked.

She stood there for a moment, as if something more was supposed to happen. So I thought of something more.

"Would you like to go out for a drink to-night?" I asked. I had not generally been so bold with women in my life, but she was attractive and we were both dead. What was there to lose?

"Tonight?"

"Tonight. Or some night."

"Sure. Some night. That'd be nice."

"Tonight?"

"Not tonight."

"But some night?"

She laughed. "Yeah. Sure. Why not?"

"I can't think of a single reason."

"How about company policy?"

"I can't think of a single other reason."

"Uh-huh."

"Anyway, I haven't been informed of an applicable policy. Do you know of any?"

"No. Not really."

"So some night it is then."

Her laugh came in a sudden and short-lived rush of musical air. No "he-he" or "ha-ha" (as if anyone actually makes those noises, though I once knew a girl who went "tee-hee") but a whoosh, and then a sort of delicate cackle after it. It didn't last long, but it made an impression on me. As did her face, and the slight curves of her small self.

"So you have nothing more to offer me as far as the Omega-Beta project is concerned?"

"No. Only that the name doesn't make sense either. But you'll get used to it. You'll get used to none of it making sense. And after that you'll even begin to understand it a bit."

"Sounds very Zen."

"I wouldn't know from Zen."

"Or Tao maybe."

"Or Tao either."

"Well thank you for your help, James. It's been enlightening."

"You're quite welcome."

She turned, maybe hesitated a moment—it pleased me to think that she did—and walked out the door.

I called after her: "And we'll go out for that drink some night."

"Yes," I heard her calling out musically from the hallway.

And why not? I was not so bad-looking a guy. I was youngish (permanently), employed (permanently?), the world was my oyster (of sorts). So let me grab some joy from this dull afterlife. Let me touch something soft and warm again and be, for a passing moment, happy.

# -15-

When did I meet my wife? I cannot remember. It might have been at work. Yes, it must have been at work. When I was washing dishes in an all-night diner and she was one of several pretty waitresses who would pass by my sink, my hose, and all those dirty plates. With the clatter of knives and forks and the murmur of talk coming through the kitchen's swinging doors, I might have asked her out for drinks one night. After a twelve-hour shift and the abuses of the service industry, who wouldn't want a drink? But when did we actually *meet*? At what point did someone stand between us and say our names, or did we do that job ourselves? That memory, which by tradition should be magical and scored with violin music, is lost to me. I can recall only that she looked young and attractive and tired in her waitress uniform. Bright red lips and too much brown eye shadow (too much being the style then). Her face was thin and nervous. Her eyes, when she had been several days without sleep, would open too wide as she stared at you, trying to understand whatever it was you were saying.

"We haven't got any more forks," was the sort of thing I would have said to her back then. "People kind of like to eat with forks," she would have answered. "They're funny that way." Then I would clear a table in the dining area and wash the small handful of forks left behind just for her.

There was a bar next door to the diner and sometimes the restaurant staff would go there for drinks after work, scaring away the gray-faced regulars who had hidden successfully for the better or worse part of the day, huddled over their drinks like they were protecting them from an imagined storm. It was a dingy, narrow place with warped wooden floors and two shifts of surly bartenders. It stank of spilled beer, sweat, pine-scented cleaning solvents and other things best left unidentified. There was a half-empty jukebox jammed into a corner and exactly two kinds of beer to choose from on tap. Perhaps a blank-faced woman in a green dress sat at a corner table.

I must have gone there once or twice with the waitress I would one day marry. I must have once or thrice looked at her face in the mirror behind the bar and thought she was beautiful. But time and memory often betray me. Dreams and plans mix themselves up with actual occurrences and then separate again inconveniently—in the middle of a sentimental reverie, in the midst of some fleeting illusion of success. A pleasant recollection sours quickly as I am forced to recall some harsher detail, or to put the event into the context of everything that comes after. Those momentous occasions of my life—first communions, first kisses, first fucks, first meeting of wife—come to me now only in gauzy and fragmented scenes. I may recall vividly and unbidden the passing glances of strangers, an inconsequential conversation at work, or the events of my brother's bachelor party. But the courtship, wooing, and seducing of my future wife and widow are extracted only with great effort. My mind's eye squints to see, but the images that come through are unclear and unreliable.

We met. I know this much is true. A drink after work seems the likeliest scenario. Then perhaps a movie. Restaurants. Dinners at her parents' home. Christmas with my family (I bought her a medallion—a full moon pressed in brass—and perfume she turned out to be allergic to). Love, or what I now must assume was once love, unfolds in a soundless, poorly shot and carelessly edited montage.

When did I ask her to marry me? I had no plan, no ring in my pocket. The idea may have grown naturally out of a conversation we had in the dark of her parents' living room or in a park one fall or winter's night. Did I actually say "Will you marry me?" or was it all somehow decided on vaguely as a good and practical idea?

We married in a courthouse in May, on a date that several embarrassments and fights have trained me to remember. I wore a used tuxedo and she a white pillbox hat and veil, and a white dress she had sewn herself. We had to wait in the hallway of the courthouse while the man before us was convicted of something. Then it was our turn, and a judge with a broken finger (I remember the splint) married us. My wife giggled nervously throughout her vows. She may not even have spoken all of the words. After the wedding we went to a movie, and the next day we were back to work. She was still a waitress and I was still a dishwasher.

That later changed. She eventually got a job in a different restaurant and then at a credit collection agency. I went to college, took some classes in communications and never graduated, but managed to finagle my way into an entry-level position at an advertising agency. The two of us grew older and fatter, moved from apartment to apartment to house, fought and fucked through several years and talked sometimes about maybe starting a family. Then I died. A car accident. The other driver's fault. And now when I tried to watch her on TV as she so effortlessly and efficiently rebuilt her life, I got only gray and white static, and I was forced to move on to other stations where the people I still remembered with love were busy living their lives.

# -16-

Something was happening to Scott. I never saw him at breakfast, and he never joined me for a beer after work anymore. For all I knew he had stopped eating and drinking altogether. On those increasingly rare occasions that I did see him slipping from his room to the front door or vice versa he seemed less *there* than he had been before. He was not thinner, but in some indefinable way he had become slighter. His skin was no longer white but seemed tinted almost blue. On his hands and arms, the darker colors of his veins seemed to float just below the surface, like dark weeds in some shallow, milky pond. His hair was wispy like thin, dead, exotic grass, and his eyes, if I chanced to look into them, were nearly translucent.

In the silence of his absence (though he had never been a noisy roommate) I heard, even in the daytime now, the sounds of other people, the way you might suddenly hear crickets and birds after some quiet but constant radio has been suddenly shut off.

When I dressed in the morning, when I soaked in the tub in the evening, when I sat down for a solitary snack at the kitchen table at any hour, I could hear people talking on the sidewalk as they passed, someone climbing or descending the stairs, water running through the pipes, light bulbs humming.

The couple next door continued to fight. The footsteps of the person above me still danced and paced and staggered.

Watching Susan and her son on TV, my brothers at work or home, or the static where my wife had once been, there was now the ever-present and growing distraction of real-life quarrels, discussions, laughter and movement around me.

But if I stopped all of my own noises for a moment to listen—if I turned off the TV, tightly closed all the faucets, planted my feet firmly and cocked my ear expectantly—the sounds stayed maddeningly just out of reach. The footsteps might stomp or dance or trip. A sound that might have been a book or a toilet seat or a bowling ball falling would drift like loosened plaster from the ceiling, growing thin and indistinct as it reached my ear.

The muddled voices were of varying tones, and I wondered how many people "lived" in this building. I had only ever seen Scott and myself, and once a fleeting glance of an old man disappearing around a corner. But now as I walked the hallway to or from my apartment I became acutely aware of the sounds and smells of other lives. The greasy brown smell of cooking, the left-behind trails of cigarette smoke, a lingering cloud of perfume. I started to walk slower and slower when I was in the hallway, hoping and fearing that I would meet someone.

The door next to our apartment, where the unhappy couple lived, remained perpetually shut, refusing to give way to the force of my stare.

The last time I saw Scott he was watching TV. Not turning to acknowledge my presence in the doorway, he held a can of beer balanced on his left knee. The can was unopened. His skin, lips, hair, and eyes had all become the same non-color.

"You've been making yourself pretty scarce," I said.

He did not even turn as he answered: "Have I?"

On TV, there were no actors playing out scenes, only a green hill of long grass, its color shifting in a soft breeze. Above the hill was a blue sky with two or three polite, white clouds crawling past a big yellow sun.

I did not disturb him further, but left him to his idyllic show.

# CLOUD 8

The next day he was not there. And the day after that. And the day after that. I opened the medicine cabinet the next nameless morning and saw one toothbrush—mine. His favorite mug was gone from the cupboard. His childhood blanket was gone from the hall closet. I opened his bedroom door and saw an empty room.

I had no roommate.

I rearranged the furniture.

# -17-

William sat at the kitchen table with his wife. In the window behind them a pink and purple evening with clouds stretched out behind silhouetted trees. They had a nice backyard. I remember sitting in it once, drinking beer while William busied himself adding fertilizer and trimming the grass that insisted on ruining the straight lines of his patio.

"Nature abhors a lawn," I told him.

Now he sat across the table from his wife. Each held a mug of something that steamed. He took a sip and made a face.

"How much salt did you put in this?" William asked her.

Maggie said: "What it said. A pinch."

William said: "What do you call a pinch?"

She held up a hand with thumb and index finger pressed together.

He looked into the mug doubtfully.

"Maybe you mixed up the salt and sugar. Maybe you got confused."

The muscles of her jaw tightened, making the flesh of her face ripple. She didn't say a word.

"Well it's brown. So at least you got the cocoa part right."

Maggie (her voice rising):"Next time you do it then."

"Don't get mad. I was just kidding."

"Maybe I'm tired of your just kidding. Don't drink it if you think it's so bad."

"It's just a little salty is all. And I don't think cocoa is supposed to be salty."

"Just throw it out and stop whining about it."

"You want me to just say it's fine? OK it's fine. It's great. Great cocoa, honey."

"Fuck you," she said quietly.

"What are you getting so worked up over?"

"You figure it out."

She stood, took her half-full mug to the sink, and slammed it down hard, hard enough to break, though for some reason it doesn't. Brown droplets splashed against the wall behind the sink. She exited the kitchen.

William (as she went up the steps): "Maggie, wait."

He stayed seated at the table. He finished his cocoa.

When he was done, he set his mug next to

hers in the sink and went up the stairs to their bedroom.

The lamps on the bedstands were off. The room was lit only by the yellow glow of the streetlight filtering in through leaves and gauzy curtains. William stood next to the bed, listening for something. Perhaps he was trying to determine if his wife was asleep. Finally, he undressed carefully and slipped into bed.

A voice came out of the shadows. It was Maggie's voice, of course, but coming as it did from the small, hidden speakers of my TV, it seemed more like a phantom—a ghost come to prick my brother's conscience.

"Why do you do that?" asked the voice.

"Do what?"

"Pick on me the way you always do."

"How do I do that?"

"You know how. Like with the hot chocolate and then all day long before that."

William, his voice rising: "What? What did I do before that?"

"What do I have to do? Make a list? You pick on me. You insult me."

"No I don't. I didn't like the cocoa. Am I supposed to say it's fine?"

"I'm not talking about the goddamn cocoa!"

He shouted: "What then?  What?"

It seemed as if he would go on, but then his head sank deeper into his pillow, and he just lay there, silently.  Light fluttered across his face, neck and chest.  The rest of the bed was in darkness.  The voice muttered something that neither William nor I could understand.

In a quiet, more reasoned tone he said: "What did you say?"

"Nothing.  I don't know why I even bother to talk to you."

He stared up at the ceiling.  Time passed.  There was the sound of breathing next to him.  It became slower and deeper.  His wife was sleeping.  There was a moist shininess to my brother's eyes.  Like our father's.  Then he closed them.

Grant Bailie

# -18-

I had never "lived" alone before.

The first apartment I ever had I shared with my brother Thomas. It was a small, two-room place in the heart of our city's seedier district, not far from the local college where Thomas and I both attended classes. The street it was on no longer exists, having been paved over several years before my death to make room for the college's new Convocation Center—which was somehow different and more expensive than an auditorium. Thomas was working as a librarian (clerk typist 2 was his official designation), and I had just started as a dishwasher. He paid most of the rent.

Our apartment had sky-blue walls darkened at about waist level—like a bathtub ring—by who knows how many dirty hips grazing or fingertips touching or asses of work pants leaning. The place smelled—the whole building smelled—of burned things, old men's liquored sweat, and mint. The beds, which came with the place and occupied the same small room, dipped in the center and creaked on rusted frames. The kitchen was small and narrow. There was an electric stove that worked sporadically, and a sink that offered water in a variety of unpredictable colors. The radiators hissed and spat out steam that bubbled the walls and floor around them, or were silent because they were not working at all and we were freezing and had to run the oven at full blast for warmth.

The two of us got along well, except on nights when I came home drunk. Thomas never drank liquor or coffee. He also didn't smoke or take cough medicine or eat American cheese. He not only did not partake in any of these things but disapproved of them all with an intense vehemence. When I came home drunk he would shake his head like a mother (our mother, who had died a few years before, could not have shaken her head with such maternal zeal) and insist on talking to me through the bathroom door while I vomited.

"And this makes you feel good?" he would ask. "This is something you wanted to do to yourself?"

I would sometimes try to answer him before being rudely interrupted by the contents of my stomach. I might try to tell him to shut up or go fuck himself. Or I might simply agree, since "uh-huh" took less time, thought, and energy.

Sober, if I inadvertently put a slice of American cheese in his sandwich, he would make a sour, disapproving face as he removed it with two careful fingers.

"What is this?" he would ask as I chewed away happily enough at my own sandwich.

"Cheese," I would say.

"This isn't cheese. This is no kind of cheese. It's the color of a traffic cone. It's like a petroleum by-product or something. They make it the same way they make plastics."

"Tasty tasty plastics," I would say as he tossed the slice into the garbage.

When he was sick, he would sniffle, cough and complain like a dying man, but would always refuse my offer of cough medicine as if I was suggesting heroin as a possible cure.

Other than these things, we got along fine.

We used to go for long walks to the better part of the city and look admiringly at the office women on their lunch hour. In the summer, we sometimes went down to the beach—fully dressed— and stared out from a bench on the boardwalk at the acres of flesh and curves.

They were idyllic days, in a way, though ones of poverty, our macaroni salad days (we both agreed on that as a cheap and viable food) that I recall with as much fondness as any time in my life.

We talked often about our romantic ideals, imagined the perfect personality and tried to attach it to one of the passing angels on the street. We made lists of the things we would do if we had that perfect girl. We reminisced about the great loves of our youth: the girl I sat behind in third grade, the girl who pushed him down in the playground in fourth grade. There was an adult theater two blocks away from our building and we sometimes went there and stayed for all three features.

When I started dating the waitress from work all that changed, as I suppose sooner or later it had to.

Though the waitress did not have the perfect qualities Thomas and I had envisioned and fantasized about, I now had someone to try and adapt these fantasies to. A practical target for all my impractical ideas. I stayed out all night sometimes, and my brother could well imagine where I was and what I was doing. We never talked about it.

She refused to spend any time at the apartment I shared with my brother because it was small, smelled bad, and was in the heart of the city's seediest district. She had a place she shared with two other women and we went there after work or after the bar.

Eventually we found a place of our own and I left my brother.

When the waitress and I agreed to marry I asked Thomas to be my best man, but he refused. He did not believe in marriage, he said, and seemed to hold it in the same regard as liquor, cigarettes, coffee, cough medicine and American cheese.

So I married in a courthouse, without a best man. Afterwards I went to a movie with my new bride, and the next day back to work.

Several years later, when my brother William married Maggie, Thomas changed, or at least softened, his position. He was the best man. At the reception he made a speech that moved everyone deeply, and brought our father and all our relatives to tears.

"I thought a lot about what I was going to say today," he said, his voice and the creased piece of paper in his hand trembling in unison, adding to the entire effect. Already my father was misty.

"Maybe some of you know the way I've felt about marriage in the past. Cynically, I guess you could say. With a . . . a jaundiced eye. But I'm thinking today . . . seeing William and Maggie . . ."

He paused to look over at them and lost his place for a second on his paper.

"But . . . seeing them . . . I feel something like a man on a sinking ship."

A quiet rumble of laughter from the audience and Thomas's nervous, oh-so- endearing smile.

If our father had been home alone watching it all on TV he would have been bawling by now, saying "Good acting" through the tears.

"The ship is sinking, and everyone is getting into the lifeboats. In couples. And here I am, cynical me, staying on the boat. I don't believe in lifeboats, you see. I have this thing . . . against lifeboats. But seeing William and Maggie, or James and his wife . . ."

Another pause to look out at his subjects, but quicker this time and with his finger holding his place on the paper.

". . . in their lifeboats . . . safe and happy in their lifeboats . . . I wonder if I haven't made a mistake. I think, at times like this, seeing my brother and his new wife, and knowing that they are truly happy, that it's good to share this world with someone else. That staying on a sinking ship is not proving any point whatsoever. So . . . I guess . . . I guess all that I'm trying to say is . . . William . . . Maggie . . ."

He folded up the sheet of paper and put it in his pocket. The rest he had memorized, or he made it up on the spot.

"I envy you. I envy you both, individually and as a couple. I hope someday that I have what you have now, and what I know you're going to have from now on. And if I can carry this apocalyptic and already overextended metaphor just a bit further . . . maybe I should start looking around for a lifeboat and someone to share it with." A murmur of approval. A pause here to smile a crooked smile. "But today . . . today . . . here's to you two. You will be very happy together."

Thomas raised his glass. Everyone in the room raised their glass in response. I wondered briefly if it was water or a soft drink in Thomas's wineglass.

"Some of the bridesmaids are available," William shouted from his seat, and everyone laughed.

The toast was over.

As the evening progressed people kept stopping by to say what a lovely job Thomas had done. I ended up drinking too much and kidded him about the speech. I told him he had not taken the metaphor far enough. He forgot to mention the stormy seas of life, the porn star sirens on the rocks, the lighthouse of religion and the lifesavers of masturbation. He took it all well enough at first but eventually he told me to shut up already. We got into a small shoving match in the parking lot. I drank too much, he told me. I told him he metaphored too much. And was self-righteous and something of a hypocrite, though in truth I had some difficulty in pronouncing the word and may have called him something else entirely.  My wife pulled on my arm and said it was time to go.  She drove.  Back to our apartment, back to our own happy little home, back to our own refuge and safe harbor from all the storms, tidal waves, and sea monsters of that cruel and temporary world.

# -19-

I could have written a book on dining in the afterlife, on the general state of its bars and restaurants (varied), the tendencies of its cuisine (fried, with cheese), and the state of its service (efficient). It would have been nice if someone had asked me—if the Abraham Lincoln in charge of guidebooks had called me into his office one day and said: "James, we have a job befitting someone with your sharp mind, your ability with people, your readiness to adapt . . ."

No one ever did, of course, and in fact I did not dine out as much as one might expect in a world that does not charge or ask for tips. Alone, I have always been more inclined to eat a sandwich over the sink than anything else, and I learned that this habit was less a condition of poverty or frugality than I would have thought.

I did, on occasion, venture out into a world where I waited to be seated in smoking or non-smoking, listened politely to the specials and then usually ordered something fried, with a cheese sauce, served between two hearty slices of "our own" fresh-baked sourdough bread.

The food was always competently cooked, competently presented, competently served—never did it rise above or fall below competent. Nor did it ever approach anything more exotic than a pesto sauce or "our own" fresh-baked sourdough bread.

The portions were reasonable. The servers wore white shirts and black bow ties, or they wore red or green polo shirts. Their pants were black or khaki.

I suppose it would have been a small, dull book had I written it. Every restaurant would have gotten the same mid-range number of stars. It would have been hard coming up with different ways to say: adequate and uninspired cooking.

There was a mall near my office. It was the usual sort of place, with skylights, a main fountain, two levels of shopping and escalators connecting them. It had three restaurants and a food court, and sometimes the less-dedicated Komacor employees would spend their lunch breaks there. I went with increasing frequency but always dined alone, since I didn't know any of the less-dedicated Komacor employees. None of them were in my department.

There was a place there that was my favorite, mostly by virtue of it being closest to the entrance. A restaurant and bar with props of generic childhood nailed to the walls or hanging from the ceiling by wires. A rusted red wagon. A tricycle. Toy trucks. A tin pail and shovel.

I asked Mary to join me there one evening after work. I had caught up with her in her office before she left and reminded her that she had promised me "some night." Night was indeed approaching, I pointed out, a night that qualified as "some."

On occasion she did her hair up in a girlish ponytail or in some more professional configuration piled on top of her head, but it was down that day, which perhaps emboldened me as much as anything. That, or her spring dress with its tiny red, green and white flowers against a dark blue background. The dress showed her legs. I liked the shape and color of them and imagined that I would also like the feel of them.

She agreed to dine with me, and while the sun was sinking behind a building, I found myself waiting for her in the small sitting area outside her office. There was a coffee table with several magazines bearing names like "Quality" and "Dynamic" and "Performance" fanned out on top of it. I picked up one and flipped through the pages, starting in the back and moving to the front to show my complete disregard for whatever it was that "Quality,"

"Dynamic" and "Performance" had to tell me. Mostly I just looked at the pictures, avoided the words (though now and then I winced at a string of them that sounded like the minutes of the last Komacor meeting), and waited for Mary.

~

We sat in a booth beneath a toy soldier suspended from a plastic parachute. Beside us badminton rackets were crossed and nailed to the wall like swords.

"There's another meeting next week," she said, playing nervously with the small pink paper umbrella sticking from her drink.

"Again?"

"A 'needs assessment' meeting, whatever that means."

"It means we are going to assess our needs, I imagine."

"I imagine so."

"But let's not talk about work." I smiled my smooth, warm, inviting smile, which I had practiced once in front of a mirror for more than half an hour when I was alive. I was hopeful that it would work better in the afterlife under poor lighting.

"OK," she said, smiling back her own warm, inviting, presumably unpracticed smile.

I studied her face for a moment. In the dim

light, her skin had a sort of glow to it, like the ghostly white that bedsheets or curtains become when your eyes have adjusted to the dark of the bedroom. Her charmingly crooked front tooth was the same shade of white. Her hair and lips and nails looked almost black in contrast.

"You going to John's party next week?" she asked.

"John?"

"From work."

"Landsdale? He's having a party?"

She hesitated, and perhaps some twinge of sympathy or embarrassment entered her expression, or showed itself in the slight narrowing of her eyes.

"Yes," she said. "I think so. I think he is."

"Hmm."

"I'm sure he'll tell you about it. I only found out because I ran into him in the lunchroom."

"I ran into him in the lunchroom yesterday. He didn't say a thing."

"Oh. Well, I'm sure he meant to invite you. He'll probably mention it tomorrow."

"Maybe I should hang out in the lunchroom until he does."

"I'm sure he'll mention it tomorrow."

"Of course."

There was music playing in the background.

Something bland and wordless that I had heard before.

"You look very nice, by the way," I said.

"Thank you."

She sipped her drink. I gulped mine. A
couple in the booth next to ours laughed about
something. The bartender turned on a novelty light
hanging from one of the walls, causing a glowing,
two-dimensional beer bottle to pour a continuous
stream of glowing two-dimensional beer into a
glowing two-dimensional mug.

"So they're going to assess our needs, are
they?" I said.

"Mm-hmm."

"Fancy that," I said. "Fancy them with their
crazy needs assessing and whatnot."

Sometime later, she said that she had to get
to bed early for work the next day. I walked her to
the corner, hovering over her for a moment there,
wondering about kissing her, waiting for some hidden force to come to me and show me the way to
her lips. But nothing came. She turned back once
to wave as she walked toward her bus, which came
without her having to wait for it.

Despite the romantic defeat, it was a pleasant night for walking. A full moon hung bright in a
sky with just enough clouds and stars to make it
interesting. Too nice a night to go home. Espe-

cially when I could walk forever without growing
tired, and when there were so many free busses and
taxis to take, and so many open bars to visit.

# -20-

I took a free taxi to an open bar, a bar that looked like every other bar in this afterlife. The same types of people filled the stools and booths and, though I drank several drinks in quick succession, I could not obtain the delusion of community or camaraderie that I sought. The faces around me gained no warmth. My focus grew less clear but no softer. My movements became clumsy and restless.

I rose from my stool, pretended to throw money on the counter in some dramatic exit gesture, and staggered to the door.

Outside, the air felt good against my face. It renewed my energy. Reborn, but not sober, I again had hope for the night, so instead of going home as I had intended when I left the bar, I crawled into the backseat of a cab that happened by and told the driver to "take me someplace interesting. Is there a good bar you know of? A good one, I mean. Someplace cheap. No cover charge. No dancing girls."

Politely ignoring the more nonsensical elements of my request, the driver smiled, tapped the wart on his nose in a knowing way, and said: "There's a place I like. On the other side of town. It's certainly interesting, I think."

"Take me there, please. Please take me there. Please. If you please."

"Yes, sir."

"Thank you. Please and thank you."

We drove for what may have been a long time, through streets that were dark and unfamiliar. Since I was talking more or less like an idiot, I decided to be quiet for a while. I slumped back into the seat and immediately fell into a long dreamless sleep. I may have slept for days, weeks or years, and when the cab stopped in front of the next nameless and neon-trimmed brick box, my drunkenness had left me. There was nothing else to do but go inside and try to find my intoxication again, or find a better, more enduring and endearing one.

The cab driver came inside with me, and while this new place seemed no different than all the others, he pointed, in a prideful way, to the long black bar, the selection of liquors and beers on tap, and the people who crowded around talking and laughing, as if it were all somehow unique and important.

The people, in fact, did seem paler than

usual, and the night outside the window more permanently black, but the rest was the same, the same clever signs hanging from wood-paneled walls, the same canoe paddles nailed on restroom doors.

We took a seat in a corner booth and ordered two drinks from a slow and nearly green waitress. Thinking it might be the lighting, I looked down at my own hand, but I was still the usual neutral beige.

"This must be the unhealthy part of town, huh?" I said when she had left.

"How do you mean?"

"Everyone seems like they're down a few pints of blood or something."

He laughed. "More than that in a few cases, I imagine."

He set his stovepipe hat on the table, leaned back, and ran a hand through his hair. Then he picked up a napkin and wiped blood from his hand.

"You're hurt!" I said, though he himself did not seem startled or concerned about it.

"Oh, it's always like that. Here, at least. It's kind of a condition."

"A condition?"

"A chronic condition. Yes."

"Eczema?"

"No."

I didn't want to stare or go through the small

list of skin diseases I could name, so instead I looked around at the other patrons. They all had conditions, as it turned out. The man in the next booth had a bullet hole between his eyes. Across from him sat a woman whose shirt was dotted with blood, which formed a smeared and random pattern against the white of her blouse. At the bar, a knife stuck out from the hunched- over back of one patron, while the person next to him demurely adjusted a scarf around the slash in her throat. In the corner an immolated woman talked to a frozen man, and I wondered how I could have failed to notice something like that when I first walked through the door. But it is like that sometimes when you enter some scene or situation for the first time; your expectations of the usual are superimposed for a brief moment over what might be truly new.

Water spilled from the shoes of the drowned man as he crossed his legs and tried to light a cigarette. ("Do you mind?" he asked his companion. "Go right ahead," she said. "The damage is done.") Patches of red soaked through fresh shirts. Exit wounds, like fatal cowlicks, disturbed the coifs of the formerly fashionable. Blood dripped from the perpetual holes of the stabbed, shot or beaten. In short, there was a violent ending in every seat, at every table, by the jukebox, and in the line to the men's room.

Some covered their various traumas with hats or scarves, but most, it seemed, wore their wounds like proud accessories, as if their lethal cuts and bruises were heirlooms, bright jewels hanging from their necks, wrapped around their wrists and arms, adorning their heads. Some of the openings, I noticed, bled freely, while others were like dark ruby portals into those parts of the human body that were never meant to know light or air.

Everywhere could be heard the general murmur of complaint. They complained about their tragic deaths and permanent wounds like someone would complain about their spouse, job or faulty water heater.

"Right in the back," I heard someone in another booth saying. "I think that's the part that gets me most. Right in the back . . ."

"Do you have any idea how much it hurts to fall down a flight of concrete steps?" someone else said.

And: "Those fucking shards. Let me tell you. If you ever get a chance to pick your own ending, pick something without glass. That's my advice to you."

I heard very little by way of response to any of these remarks, nothing much more than "I can imagine," and "Tell me about it," and I was reminded of certain conversations I had had in the past with people who did not listen so much as more or less politely wait their turn to talk.

"Are you from here?" I asked my cab driver.

"Used to live here," he said. "Not anymore, but I like to come back now and then.    Keep in touch with my roots, so to speak."

"Your hometown," I said.

"Something like that."

As gruesome a scene as it was, with all these limping cadavers grousing about their deaths, or their killers, or the supernatural trouble they now had with laundry, I found it strangely comforting. Here was a place that made some mention—in its fashion—of the life before this, and of the sudden shock in which some of us had left it.   At last I had found a place that wasn't glossed over with the meaningless tasks of a meaningless job and a missing roommate who avoided every question put to him.

The waitress brought our drinks.  She tried to smile but her jaw appeared to be broken.  I thanked her.  I would have liked to leave her a tip.

I drank my beer while the cab driver sipped a decidedly unpresidential strawberry daiquiri. We did not speak much, but looked at the people around us, me with discreet curiosity, him with a broad, nostalgic smile.

When he finished his drink he stood up, put

on his hat and said he needed to get back to work. I decided to stay, and thanked him for the ride.

I cannot say how long I sat there drinking and looking. My empty glasses were replaced efficiently with full ones by the same green waitress while the sky remained black outside the bar's one window.

The alcohol took effect again, but in a quieter way than before. I suppose it was some degree of sentimentality that held me there—some morbid brand of nostalgia that made me see, in the gaping wounds of others, the beauty and sadness of my own passing. I longed for a conversation with one of them, and struggled for an opening line that might break the ice. But even in life I had had difficulty with those connections that come so casually to others, so it was even harder for me to now walk up to that pretty woman at the bar and say, "speaking of sucking chest wounds or blunt head trauma . . ."

Speaking of that pretty woman at the bar: I recognized her. It was, of course, a little difficult to look past the horizontal slashes still open at both wrists, or her deathly pallor and the cloudy glaze of her eyes, but there was something about her that was familiar. It stood on the edge of my brain, threatening to dive into consciousness. Where had I seen her? Her hair was dark and straight, her nose small and slightly turned up. Her forehead seemed almost preternaturally large. Her lips were a bluish red, a purplish blue, a reddish purple.

She did not sit at the bar, but stood there waiting for her order. After she received it—something pastel and frozen with an impaled cherry on the top—she began walking in my direction.

She was almost past me when I said her name out loud.

"Pamela Bennett."

She stopped and smiled curiously down at me. I could see her mind working, rifling through the photo album or Rolodex or supercomputer that was her memory to find a face that in some way correlated with mine. She looked about ten years older than the last time I had seen her, and I would have looked about twice that much older myself.

"James?" she said finally, and I felt happy and relieved.

"Are you here with anyone?" I asked, looking pointedly at the empty seat across from me.

She shook her head and sat down.

"It's been awhile," she said, studying my face for . . . what? Attraction? Age? Signs of death?

"An eternity, practically," I said. "It's good to see you again."

"Even under these sad circumstances," she

said with mock weariness, as if reciting it to the ninety-ninth person in line at her funeral. In a surprisingly casual gesture, she held her wrists up for me to see. Thankfully, the blood did not spill out but only glimmered darkly within the gaps of her flesh.

"Self-inflicted?" I asked. What else could I say? This kind of thing seemed to be a topic of casual conversation here.

"Of course. The only way to go."

"I'm sorry."

She shrugged. "The things we do for love."

"Yes."

"What about you? Poison?"

I looked down suspiciously at my beer and back at her.

"No thanks?"

"I mean *were* you poisoned?" she said. "Die in your sleep? Suffocated by a pillow? Heart attack? Though I admit, I've never met anyone around here who succumbed to a heart attack."

"Car accident."

She seemed surprised. "Really? Must have been a pretty gentle one. Air bag?"

"I don't recall the details exactly. I don't think air bags were involved."

"Curiouser and curiouser."

She sipped her drink and I, feeling the need

to return to that point where we had both shared the world together, said: "You were in drama."

"Yes?"

"I saw you try out for a play once. 'Our Town.' Or 'The Music Man'."

"The only two plays our school ever did. I was in marching band too. I played the flute."

"I never saw the marching band."

"We played at every game."

"I never went to a game. I liked you in drama though. I thought you were very good. You wanted to go to New York, didn't you?"

"Yes. To play the flute."

"No . . ."

"No. To be an actor, of course. I was there for a couple of years. Then I fell madly, deeply, truly in love." She touched the slit on one wrist—wistfully, I thought, the way one fingers the edges of old photos.

"You know, I didn't do it right," she said.

"What?"

She pointed to one of her wrists. "I cut horizontal. Very amateurish. I have since learned from people who know that the really serious ones cut vertical. Much more efficient and hard to repair that way. I knew the trick of a warm bath, of cutting my wrists in water the same temperature as my body so that the blood doesn't shut off in shock right away or something, but no one told me about the vertical versus horizontal bit. It's very embarrassing. Branded as an amateur for eternity."

"Horizontal seems to have worked sufficiently well for you," I said.

"Yes. Well, the bath helped."

~

I went home with her, staggering alongside her to her apartment in a nearby tall and featureless building. All of the windows of her living room overlooked a factory across the street, a tall, thin smokestack rising from its center, ending in a blue-yellow flame that flickered against the black sky. I fell asleep on her couch watching the flame, listening to her tell me of the pink ring her dying had left behind in the tub.

When she woke me up the next day, the sky was still black, but the flame, as if in some harbinger or replacement of morning, burned more brightly.

For lack of a better idea, I went to work with her. Her job was at the factory outside her window. Standing at the assembly line of the living dead, attaching nuts and bolts to small brass blocks. When we were done the sky was still black (or was it black again?). We went back to the same bar as the previous night. (Day?)

"I considered pills," she told me over drinks.

"I saw you in 'Our Town'," I told her. "You were very good."

The rest of the night went on in much the same way. In the morning I went with her back to the factory. After work we went to the same bar again, sitting in what had now become our usual booth. Then back to her apartment for more words, sleep, and back to work again.

Over coffee one morning, she recited her suicide note from memory. Over drinks one evening she told me of the difficulties she had in slitting her second wrist, and the care she had taken in choosing the proper knife (nothing so tacky as a steak knife or cumbersome as a cleaver).

Over coffee one day she said. The day after that she said. That morning, that evening, I said, she said . . . But in fact, I never saw the sun rise or fall or even appear. There was only the factory flame burning bright in the sky, like an industrial-strength holy ghost. There was coffee at a kitchen table in the beginning and drinks in a booth at the end and a conveyor belt connecting the two that carried us daily, weekly, monthly, yearly, eternally, from one point to the other.

I wish I could offer some simple explanation for why I stayed. Pamela and I did not kiss, I slept on the couch, and our conversations were one-sided at best. It was as if I had fallen asleep on a bus again, missed the stop to my regular world, and was unable to find my way back.

One day my chest began to hurt—a dull force pushing against my sternum with a steady increase in pressure. Examining myself in the bathroom mirror I discovered a vague and purplish circle in the center of my chest, like the emblem of some poorly focused superhero. Bruise Man. But what strange new power was this?

The next day my right eye became swollen and red, and I lost the ability to see clearly out of it.

The next morning—for convenience let me call it morning—I said: "I should be getting back." I had found broken glass in my pockets and the bruise on my chest was beginning to take on the distinctive shape of a steering wheel.

She looked up from her coffee (or from her wrist?).

Her face did not appear overly sad, distraught, brokenhearted, relieved, indifferent, or any one of the other myriad half-dozen emotions I have had the pleasure of seeing cross a woman's face when I decided to leave. I could not tell what she felt, though I felt fairly certain she would not be re-slitting her wrists over me.

"How come?" she asked.

"I should. Don't you think? I have a job.

They gave me an apartment."

She shrugged. "If you think," she said.

"I think."

"Well, it was good seeing you again, James."

"It was good seeing you again, Pamela," I said, tilting my head to look at her with my one good eye.

"I'll miss you," she said, but I knew that she was only being polite.

An uninjured Abraham Lincoln drove the cab that picked me up in front of her apartment. I got in the back, nodded hello and said "home." Then I closed my eyes.

By the time I reached my building the sun had risen. Pigeons cooed on the sidewalks, ledges and rooftops. A couple of the more ambitious ones were even singing in the trees—at least they were making that extended, low, one-note warble that passes for song in the pigeon world.

"Hang on a few minutes," I told the driver. I went inside to change my clothes and splash some water on my face and under my arms. When I came back out the cab was still there. I climbed into the back and said: "I guess you better take me to the Komacor building."

# -21-

Upon returning, it seemed that I had only been gone for a day, or at most a long weekend. I had been missed, but not greatly so. The same three security guards were struggling with the same crossword puzzle in the lobby. The same people—familiar but nameless—rode the elevator with me, getting off at their usual floors, exchanging their usual pleasantries. Sitting at my desk I found the same papers in my in-box and the same words waiting for me on my computer screen.

I had been in my office the better part of the morning when John Landsdale finally tapped on my doorframe and said: "We missed you yesterday." It was said casually, but not warmly.

"Sick," I explained. And hadn't I been? Had there not been aches and pains, bruises and blood?

"Really," he said, looking only slightly less skeptical than if I had called off with a case of stigmata.

"Pinkeye," I explained, pulling the lower lid

of my eye down in an offer of proof. Fortunately, it was still bloodshot enough in the corners to be cause for concern.

"I see." He took a step backwards. "Isn't that contagious?"

"Not this kind."

"Still . . ." He closed my office door as he backed out of the room.

For the rest of the day I was left to my own devices, and to the hopelessly nonspecific manual for those devices.

*With Omega-Beta as your tool of choice, even the most labor-intensive tasks will be reduced to a few simple steps.   With an ease of use and clarity of function formerly missing from office products of a similar, if less complete, nature, you will find . . .*

And on and on and on.

# -22-

Thomas was washing his dishes. He had let them soak, judging by the foul, dark water in the sink, for more than a week. Pale and bloated bits of unidentifiable food floated facedown on the surface. If he waited another few days, everything would break down into a thin, beige layer of scum. But Thomas was tackling the problem before this could happen, scrubbing away at pot and pan (he had only one of each) and assorted (unmatched) silverware and dishes with a sponge that was nearly black with some process of mold and decay best left unexamined.

He shared the apartment with three cats, and it was the loose, stray hair of these pets that danced along in every beam of sunlight, collecting in all corners and upon all flat surfaces. White, black and brown clumps, loosely held together in balls, drifted across the floor with the occasional breeze. Other solid and stationary constructions, coughed up and forgotten, weighed down the stacks of paper strewn about every room—unsent or un-answered letters, half-filled-out tax forms, outdated newspapers and all the other odd ends of ephem-eral that crowded my brother's life and apartment.

When I lived with him, Thomas had been a neat and exacting roommate, but on his own he lived in clutter and filth. Once every month or so he tried to straighten things up, but became bogged down in some minor part of the process: alphabetizing books, arranging his records chronologically, sort-ing his pornography in order of preference, genre, sub-genre—blonde, brunette or redhead. Inevita-bly he never finished the greater task.

When I was alive, I would visit him from time to time and kid him about his squalor. It was the sort of mess they mentioned in obituaries, I told him, with city workers or landlords exaggerating—though perhaps only slightly—about having to wade through ankle-deep animal feces, or cover their face with a handkerchief to stand the stench. Sometimes I tried to help him clean up, but I too would be over-whelmed by the enormity of the task and become distracted by some lesser chore. The two of us would end up taking a break that lasted the rest of the day. We would eat pizza, watch TV, leaf wist-fully through his girly magazines, and talk once again about the things we would do for and with our ideal girl.

# CLOUD 8

When Thomas was in love—which would happen every few months or so—his apartment became an impediment, a barrier, a mission and a metaphor. He would skip a night's sleep to clean, and while cleaning he would dream about the things he could do in a perfect apartment with the perfect girl.

But it was never finished, never cleaned. The various and varied loves of his life came and went, sometimes consummated (sometimes among the filth and clutter and floating hair), but never staying for good.

Now he left the dishes to dry in the rack and let the water out of the sink. An orange-brown film was left behind in the white sink.

He made himself toast and Nutella and took it to the other room to eat in front of the TV. He did not use a plate. The crumbs fell upon his lap.

Some show that may have come into existence after I left his world was playing (I did not recognize any of the characters or actors).

On his small TV ghosts haunted every object with a milky echo. A handsome young man and beautiful young woman and their ghosts sat on an empty beach. Sweaters were draped over shoulders, and a woolen blanket was spread out in the sand beneath them, giving the impression, despite the lack of vegetative evidence, that it was autumn.

Grant Bailie

A cool, brisk wind carefully mussed their youthful and beautiful hair.

A wobbly red sun sank like a giant valentine heart into a deep blue envelope of ocean as they talked about love and commitment. They laid out—with sweeping gestures and earnest eyebrows—their grand designs for the future, when the young man's career as a bold, intense and rebellious artist started to pay off, and the woman's burgeoning career as a model continued to burgeon. But there was the hint of growing conflict too; some dark beast loomed over the horizon even as the last of the sun's fiery glory was swallowed by the sea.

The young man did not like the way one photographer (a recovering alcoholic) had been looking at his model girlfriend. The young woman had similar reservations about her boyfriend's beautiful art studio assistant (a recovering sex addict). But that woman meant nothing to him, he assured her. Nothing. Just as the photographer meant nothing to her. And so they kissed beneath the violet sky, and held each other tight. But what was that strange faraway look the beautiful model made over her lover's broad shoulder? Dusk's dark light played ruefully against it, and even the violin section of a nearby orchestra could tell that something was up.

~

# CLOUD 8

William and Maggie were sitting in folding chairs on their patio. It was a summer evening. They were dressed lightly, and the day still hung softly onto the edges of the sky. Long, dark shadows crossed their backyard. The yellow light over the back door was switched on. The neon blue light of a bug-zapper hummed at the corner of their patio and crackled suddenly with the death of some hapless gnat.

Maggie lit a cigarette, drew from it and let the smoke out slowly.

"How many is that today?" William asked.

"Was I supposed to be counting?"

"You were supposed to be quitting."

"I said I was cutting back. Not quitting."

"Cutting back then."

"I am."

"How do you know if you're not counting?"

"I smoked less today than yesterday. I'll bring an abacus with me tomorrow if that'll make you happy."

"That would make me happy," he said. She made a face that seeped smoke from between her teeth and in two vaporous tusks from her nostrils.

"I live to make you happy," she said.

He looked at his watch.

"Is there anything good on TV tonight?" he asked.

~

My sister Susan and her husband sat in their small, toy-cluttered living room watching TV. They were watching the same show as my brother Thomas, but on a better and clearer screen. The handsome young artist was creating something big and colorful in his studio. His beautiful assistant watched wistfully from behind a ladder as the artist so skillfully, so boldly, so sexily (a sweat-dampened curl of hair fell across his forehead) splashed, brushed, slathered and dripped his colors across an enormous blank canvas. A painting evolved in a montage set to the tune of the latest timeless song: blood-red sun dripping, flesh-colored clouds, a black jet trailing fire across a pink sky, a screaming disembodied mouth. What a dark soul the handsome young artist had (so said the look in the assistant's clear blue eyes). What a troubled mind lay beneath his bronzed and lantern-jawed surface.

Little Robert was asleep in his bed. He was bigger now. His yellow hair had darkened to brown. His round, cherubic face had lengthened to something less babyish and more boyish. His eyes were closed, his breath soft and slow from between his dark lips, slightly open, shaped into a kiss. A nightlight on the dresser swirled a pattern of stars, moons and a cow over his bedroom walls and ceiling.

"Goodnight, Robert," I said out loud in my

empty apartment.  I turned off the TV and went to bed.

# -23-

Mary looked beautiful in the sunlight. There are women like that, who are merely pretty or cute in the fluorescence of the office, or under the much-fabled and sung about moonlight, but who, in the bright yellow light of day, with a slight breeze lifting up the ends of their soft hair or the edges of their skirt, take on a new attractiveness that can only be described as beautiful. It is not so simple a matter as saying that they look better in this light, or worse in the other. There is an actual metamorphosis taking place. They are in their element, a flower opening up I might say, if I were the sort of person to say a thing like that.

We were going to a cafe down the street from our building, a casual place with casually dressed waiters and a generic menu. John Landsdale had recommended it to her, and she suggested it to me when I asked if she was doing anything for lunch.

She wore a short spring dress (it was always

a spring dress) and walked in a bouncing, happy manner. Not for the first time did I notice the pleasant flair of her hips, the outward curve of her breasts, the fact that she was several inches shorter than myself.

They gave us a table in the corner and we ordered coffee and sandwiches. I was happy that a piece of sunlight from the front window fell across the room and caught the edge of her face when she leaned forward to pick up her cup or sandwich.

"Still not invited to John's party," I told her.

"Oh it's just a small thing," she said after a moment. "I think he only invited me because I was nearby when he was talking about it. Just to be polite, you know?"

"Maybe he doesn't like me." I smiled to show that it was only a joke, or at least, something of no great concern to me. "Anyway, I'm not much for parties."

We chewed and sipped for a bit without talking. The light reflected off her water glass and threw little bits of it shimmering against her skin and hair.

"You look very nice today," I said.

She smiled.

"What do you think would happen if I stole a car?" I asked her. Her smile did not exactly falter, though I think it may have teetered for a moment on the edge of faltering.

"I beg your pardon?"

"Do you think there are police here? I mean, how far do you think I would get?"

"Are you serious?"

"No. Not serious. Just curious. Seriously curious. I wonder about things sometimes."

"Well I haven't seen any police. But let's go steal a car and find out."

"Are *you* serious?"

She laughed. "No!"

"Me neither."

We finished eating and went back to work.

At my office a man was kneeling in the doorway with a yellow tape measure laid out against the floor.

"What's going on?" I asked him.

"Measurements," the man said, mostly to the floor. "We're doing some remodeling tomorrow."

"No kidding." He moved aside a little to give me room to enter. "New carpet?"

"Eventually. Tomorrow we just tear down the walls."

I sat down behind my desk and stared at him.

"And then you put new walls up, right?" I asked.

"No," he said.

He rolled up his tape measure, put it in his pocket and left.

I stared at the walls of my office for a minute. They seemed new, unscarred, neutral-colored and generally inoffensive. I rather liked them being there. It made it seem more like an office.

I went back to work deleting, replacing, renaming, merging. The sky darkened. A star appeared.

That night I dreamt that I was flying again. But from a great height, so that all of the world that I once knew was far away and abstract: a living map of farmlands, highways, streets, and the roofs of houses. I stayed firmly above it all as colors shifted across the folds and scars of a blue, green and brown planet. Where was my father's house? My parents' graves? William and Maggie's well-maintained yard? Thomas's apartment building? The playground that Susan and her husband took my nephew Robert to? From so high and far away nothing seemed real.

The next day the walls were gone from my and all the other offices on the 42$^{nd}$ floor. The floors were left as bare concrete, with bright orange markings in spray paint indicating where carpet would one day be laid. Sitting at my desk I could look across an expanse of desks that stretched out in front of me in an almost endless line. I waved at

Mary at her desk, about a hundred yards from mine. We were facing each other, as we had been, I realized, when there had been walls between us.

She waved back with an amused smile and walked over to where I sat.

"Something, huh?" she said.

"It's ridiculous."

"The carpet is going to be put in tomorrow."

I could only shake my head in disbelief. It was like a school room, only one that had been stretched out to some epic scale, with the desks turned at a variety of angles, as if following the latest modern teaching plan designed to encourage independent study and teamwork dynamics.

Mary said: "The good news is that the needs assessment meeting has been canceled."

"How's that good? I finally feel like I have some needs that could use some assessing."

"Like what?"

"Well my office could really use some walls, for one thing. Just off hand, that's something."

She laughed, tapped a knuckle on my desk as a sign of support or sympathy, or as a period at the end of the conversation, and went back to her own desk.

"I am definitely needing some walls here," I called after her.

A few other faces looked up from their

desks. I saw Marge Boyton in the distance. I saw John Landsdale. I saw Steven Roth. They frowned at me disapprovingly. I was not contributing a positive influence to the team dynamic.

I got up, lifted my desk, and turned it so that it faced the window, which was something, I hoped, they could not remove.

# -24-

Susan and little Robert walked hand in hand down a sidewalk. It was autumn: there were orange, red and brown leaves on the trees, sidewalks and grass. The sky was blue except at the horizon— or what could be seen of the horizon between houses and trees—where a slate gray wall of clouds was advancing slowly. A breeze rattled the branches and more leaves came fluttering to the ground. Robert was wearing a backpack, and on it was a cartoon character unfamiliar to me, with a large pink head and big blue eyes.

There were many children on the sidewalk; some walked with their mothers or fathers, some with other kids, some on their own. They all went in the same direction: down the sidewalk, around the corner, past a cluster of saplings with blood-red leaves, over the spot where the sidewalk had been raised and broken by the roots of an old tree, on into the parking lot that surrounded the school.

Already the children were lining up by the

door. Susan kissed her son on the top of his head and then on his lips as he turned his face up to her. Crouching down so that her eyes were level with his and her hand was on his shoulder, she pointed him toward the line. He took his place at the end. His mother took a step backward and Robert's face instantly began to tremble. My sister—his mother—chewed on her lip.

The teacher came out and greeted her new students in exaggerated and syrupy tones. They were going to have a great time today, she told them. She had many fun games and treats in store for them, if they would just follow her inside.

The line began—with tiny, awkward steps, with backs bumping fronts and little hands pushing and tugging—to enter the building.

Other parents, smiling with pride or grimacing in sympathy, took still pictures and videos of this momentous event.

There was a sudden commotion as Robert turned and rushed back to his mother's arms. She hugged him, kissing the wetness on his cheeks, then picked him up and carried him to the doorway, where the last of the children were entering. She set him down and petted his hair.

"You'll be fine, Robert," she said. "You'll have fun. I bet you'll even make some new friends today."

He appeared less than convinced as, with one more backwards glance and several more halting steps, he entered the school.

~

William sat at his desk. He worked in a brightly lit office answering phone calls or making them. At the same time he was always doing something on his computer: going over figures, following the transport of some product or another, updating his customer base, playing solitaire. He was separated from his nearest coworker by a portable wall that rose shoulder-length in front of and at one side of his desk. He had various cartoons and slogans tacked onto the wall. "The only difference between this place and the Titanic is that the Titanic had a band," one of them said. "He doesn't have to shoot me now, shoot me later," said another.

"Believe me, Mr. Hauser," he was saying to the phone. "No one is more anxious for that to arrive than myself. I've been tracking it all week and it should be there by this afternoon."

He listened for a bit, then picked up a coffee mug that left behind a wet brown ring on a stack of papers. He took a sip. The mug said: "Go ahead—Make My Day!" Underneath the slogan was a drawing of a large gun.

"No, thank *you* for your patience, Mr.

Hauser. And thanks again for doing business with us."

He hung up the phone, hit a few buttons on his keyboard and took another sip from his mug.

"Who wants to grab some lunch with me?" he shouted out to no one in particular.

"A bit early, isn't it?" a voice said from the other side of the cubicle wall.

"Brunch then. Mr. Hauser has a way of making me hungry." Apparently this passed for a joke in the office: there was the sound of laughter from behind the wall.

A girl appeared from around the corner and leaned one hip against my brother's desk.

"Brunch sounds good," she said.

William looked up and smiled.

She was a pretty girl, and his smile acknowledged this. She was young (21 or so—a decade or two younger than my brother, at any rate), with blue hair like cotton candy, a small upturned nose and bee-stung red lips. She wore a black T-shirt and a plaid, schoolgirl's dress, white socks, and black running shoes. The outfit seemed designed to exaggerate her youth while drawing attention to the subtle yet distinctive curves of her body, and the smoothness of her white legs which, in fact, seemed younger than any other part of her.

"Brunch it is then," William said.

~

My brother Thomas sat behind a desk at the library. A line of people stood before him with their stacks of books ready to be checked out. He ran a scanner over the back tags of two books on modern warfare and handed them back to the elderly man in the front of the line. A young man stepped forward and handed Thomas another stack of books. Thomas nodded politely and ran the scanner across the backs of the books.

The next person in line was a young woman. She smiled as she set the books down. My brother smiled back.

"Good book," he said as he scanned the back.

"You've read it?" she asked.

"A long time ago."

~

Little Robert sat at a round table around which children his own age were gathered in boy-girl-boy-girl pattern. There were several other tables set up in this same manner. The teacher stood in front of the class and held up a red crayon.

"Can anyone tell me what color this is?" she asked.

The girl next to Robert, a little girl in a flower dress and blonde hair tied up in pigtails, raised her hand.

"Brittany," the teacher said. "Can you tell me what color this is?"

"Red!" Brittany said.

"Very good," the teacher said, smiling broadly.

"It's red!" Robert shouted.

~

William sat at a table in a diner with the girl with blue hair. She was eating scrambled eggs and toast and drinking coffee. He was eating a sandwich and drinking coffee.

"I've been getting all the nut-jobs today," she said.

"Must be the full moon," he said.

"In broad daylight?"

"It's out and full somewhere, right?"

She laughed. "I guess. Somewhere."

"So how do you like the job so far? Besides the nut-jobs, I mean."

"I like it." She nodded and repeated for emphasis. "I like it."

"Everyone treating you OK?"

"Oh sure. Everyone is great."

"Really? Even Karen?"

She smiled and looked down at her coffee. "She is a bit . . . um . . . standoffish, isn't she?"

"Yes, but don't let that fool you. She's really a grade-A bitch once you get to know her."

She nearly choked on her coffee.

"You're funny," she said.

"Oh now," my brother said mock-sheep-
ishly.

"No, really. You're always making me
laugh."

"Well thanks, I guess."

"You're my favorite person in the office, you
know." She smiled (a come-hither smile?).

"Really now, you're going to swell my poor
head. But I like you too."

More smiles exchanged and a moment of silence. They sipped their coffee.

"I probably shouldn't tell you this, but I was
sorry when I found out you were married."

"So was I," William said.

~

But always the girl is pretty or beautiful, it
seems I am saying, and sooner or later you must
question my judgment. But to me it is true; they
are always pretty and beautiful.

Beauty is not such a rare thing as people
would have you believe. In the afterworld or the
one before it, I could not go to the grocery store,
the post office, the bus stop without seeing some
line and color of flesh, some shape of brow or nose
or chin, some glint of eye or hair or teeth, that did

not stir in me some happy melancholia that is my inevitable response to beauty. It may have been lust, love, envy, disappointment or want that rose painfully from my heart, but it was always beauty that made it rise.

My brothers and I shared a similar and expansive taste in women. We liked the soft round girls or the gaunt pale ones. We liked the kind faces, the arrogant faces, the nervous faces. Exotic, or achingly common. I loved a girl once who, when she was anxious, chewed her lower lip until it bled. I loved a girl who would walk naked in fountains, and another who would not change clothes with the lights on. The admittedly limited history of the bodies I had known intimately was still one of some variety, and if I had truly known all that I desired, it would have been more varied still. The girl with her cotton candy blue hair had her kind of beauty, as did the brown-haired girl I worked with, the suicide I briefly lived with, the anonymous red-haired girl I passed on the street yesterday, the girl at Thomas's Library, the little girl who sat next to Robert in school, and once even, I suppose, the black-haired woman I married.

# -25-

During the night, they laid the carpets (grayish blue) and brought in potted plants. The furniture—desks, file cabinets, and a coffee counter—were organized into straight rows, with fifty feet or so between every object. The first thing I did upon arriving to work that morning was turn my desk back toward the window again.

A man came by and put a red piece of paper down in front of me. I looked at the desks behind me and saw that they all had red pieces of papers on them as well. The man continued down the line in front of me, putting red sheets on every desktop.

I read the red piece of paper:

*Understanding . . .*
*Taking Ownership*
*Become an informed owner of your team!*
*Learn:*

- *How ownership works.*

- *How to decide when to exercise your ownership options.*
- *How to make your decisions as part of the team dynamic.*
- *How to manage the actualities of today.*
- *How to be both a savvy team player and a thoughtful owner.*
- *How to use integrity without competition.*

*A mandatory seminar on this and other relevant topics will be held tomorrow evening in the Komacor Auditorium (located in the lower lobby, level C).*

*Please attend.*

I placed the paper on top of some other papers and began to work, but the paper was such an annoyingly and insistently bright shade of red that it kept pulling my eyes back toward it. I opened a drawer, put the paper in there, and closed it.

"You've moved your desk," John Landsdale said.

I looked up to see him standing there, his pale, shadowy form almost wavering in the air. His knuckles, thin flesh stretched tightly over white bones, tapped lightly on my desk. I had the sudden passing image of them shattering like porcelain against my desk.

"I like to have a bit of a view when I work," I explained. "It helps me concentrate."

"A great deal of planning went into the arrangement we have, you know."

"Did it?"

"Yes. A great deal."

"I can move it back if you want."

"I want that. I would like that. That's what I want."

"OK."

He didn't move. Eventually I got the idea that he wanted me to move it back right then and there. I stood up and pushed my desk back to where it was.

"Thank you," he said, and finally turned away.

I watched him leave, a phantom of a man vibrating in the air as if he were walking off into the desert, swallowed up by the heated air. Suddenly I hated him. The roundness of his shoulders, the thinness of his hair, the blandness of his features— all seemed to me at that moment a perfect illustration of the loathsomeness of his nature. It was not simple weakness; I have never been one of those men who held weakness or frailty in contempt. But there was a certain air of corruption in his anemia.

He reminded me of the final watered-down scion of a long and decadent line of tyrants, the non-participating host yawning through orgies and massacres. A man like that would drink the blood of virgins for their vitamins and iron.

He walked over to Mary and sat jauntily (or his own weak impersonation of jauntily) on the corner of her desk. Mary looked up and smiled her usual smile as he leaned forward and whispered something in her ear. They both laughed quietly— a continuation of some personal joke between them, I imagined. I felt a pang of something not quite strong enough to be jealousy, something related in some distant way to the dread of imminent failure.

I returned to my own screen for a moment, erased a word and wrote another word meaning the same thing in its place.

Looking out into the expanse of desks and workers, I saw Marge Boyton staring back at me. Her face held the sort of absent expression some people get when they have been watching an interesting scene of violence or conflict, and have not yet turned their eyes away, even after whatever tragic sight that had held their interest has calmed, disappeared or rounded a corner.

I nodded at her, on the off chance she could see me. She did not nod back. Behind her, Steven Roth sat at his desk, busily typing away at his computer. Around them a myriad of indistinct office faces chatted, sipped coffee, filed, divided files into separate files, merged files into larger files, combined this with that, divided that into this, and that. Everyone was contentedly contributing to the team dynamic.

Turning my head over one shoulder as I leaned back in my chair, I could still peek out the nearest window and see the city below and the clear blue sky above. Windows and the silver-pointed tops of buildings caught and reflected the sun like water.

Walking home after work that evening, the streets and sidewalks seemed less crowded, the leaves on the trees sparser and less green. Fewer busses passed by in the street. Fewer taxis slowed by the curb to see if I wanted a ride. Was it a holiday? Was there a change of season? The sky was gray and it began to rain.

At home, I drank beer and watched TV.

My brother William was driving the girl with the blue hair somewhere.

"So blue isn't your natural color?" my brother said and the girl laughed (she was always laughing; my brother always made her laugh; he was so funny, my brother William).

"No, and I wasn't born with my belly button pierced either."

"Whoa," said William. "That too, huh? Any tattoos?"

"Just one. A small one on my back. A little sun and moon."

"That's two."

"I got them both at the same time."

"Still . . ."

"They kind of go together."

"OK."

"Anyways, it hardly even counts. It's not like someone is going to see them."

"Even in the summer?"

"I burn easily. Intimate moments maybe."

"Ah."

"I'll show it to you sometime."

"Ah," he said again and I watched the thoughts working themselves within his face, banging around inside his head like animals trapped in a bag. His eyebrows raised and lowered. His jaw clenched and unclenched. He blinked thrice and a small, closed-lipped smile worked itself across his mouth. He checked the speedometer, the odometer, the tachometer.

"I might get another one on my ankle," the girl said. "A rose or something."

"Such a modern girl."

She made an exaggerated pout with her pink-red mouth and said: "Don't call me that."

"Modern?"

"Girl."

"Well," said my brother carefully. "You do have certain girl-like qualities."

She made a face that wrinkled her chin as she stared at him. A girl-like face.

"Good qualities," he went on. "And you are young . . ."

"I haven't been a girl for ages," she said. "I haven't been young for ages either."

"You're young enough to be the daughter I never had if I had been having the sex I never had when I was old enough to become your father."

She laughed at this and said: "You are *so* funny. Turn left at the next light. I'm not that young. And you're not that old."

"And I'm not that funny."

"You are."

"But not old? You don't think?"

"You don't act it."

"I don't have any tattoos."

"Like that has anything to do with it. It's the next building. With the red car in front."

My brother slowed his car to a stop in front of a red car parked at the curb.

"Thanks for the ride," the blue-haired girl said smiling warmly.

"My pleasure."

She paused before opening the door.

"I'm not a girl, you know," she said quietly.

"Yes. I am acutely aware of this."

She leaned toward him, her face turned up. He leaned over, and it was the moment that I had hoped for with Mary. The moment when the kiss is inevitable, germane. It did not last long and the details of it were obscured by face and hair. When it was done she straightened up, opened the door and smiled back at my brother with the sort of open affection—worship, almost—that I have sometimes dreamed of but cannot recall ever seeing, even when I was married.

"Thanks," she said.

"You're welcome," William said.

~

Thomas sat alone in a movie theater. On the screen a man walked with a slow and deliberate stride along a crowded sidewalk. Oblivious people pushed by him. Indifferent signs hung above his head. Liquor. Food. XXX Girls. Hourly Rates. Modern, Fire-Proof Rooms. A saxophone played a rambling series of notes. Scales abstracted, like the music lessons of a gifted and disturbed child. The sound of loneliness, one could imagine the director telling the composer—the sound of a man alone against the world.

# Grant Bailie

The music stopped in the middle of a note. The man stopped walking and turned around slowly. Why has the music stopped, he must have been thinking. A close shot of his eyes narrowing, an attractive wrinkle in his brow.

"Something's not right," the man said in a hoarse whisper intended for no one save himself and the audience.

Suddenly, a storefront he had just passed exploded in a fireball. Glass, fire, smoke, debris flew out in slow motion. The man, a wall of fire unrolling behind him, leapt through the air, silhouetted by the flames, propelled forward by the blast. Gumballs and glass shards brightly peppered the air.

He flew. Arms spread, face fiercely grimaced, he flew, landing face-first upon the pavement, the bright and sparkly bits raining down around him. He returned to his feet and things returned to normal speed as he looked back ruefully at the burning rubble. From one attractive cut on his brow a thin line of red trickled.

"Son-of-a-bitch will pay," he said, and the saxophonist—as if suddenly nudged awake—began to wail a long and twisting note, drowning out the approaching sirens.

# -26-

The Komacor auditorium was a cavernous place with a high, shadowy ceiling, dim red-velvet walls and descending rows of burgundy seats. Red carpet aisles sloped toward a wooden stage lit by hidden spotlights. A steady—and mandatory—stream of Komacor employees entered, and before long the place was filled with several hundred men and women and a dozen or so Abraham Lincolns (their stovepipe hats set thoughtfully on their laps).

I sat near the back, next to no one I knew, and looked for Mary, hoping she would see me and, of her own accord, take the empty seat to my right.

But the lights grew dim, and the seat to my right was taken by a man who smelled of an aftershave that reminded me of fermented gasoline. A distant figure walked out to the center of the stage.

"I bet you're wondering why I've gathered you all here today," he said, and there was a quiet rumble of polite laughter.

He was a short, stocky man with red hair

that, from my vantage point in back, was the only distinguishable characteristic of his face. Everything else was a blur of pink flesh and red mouth.

"Don't worry," he said, and I could just make out the white teeth of a broad, friendly smile. "I won't keep you long. I know you all have projects you're anxious to get back to, but maybe what I have to say here today will help you with those projects. Maybe it will help you focus a little on what's really important."

He paused—a dramatic pause, I supposed, though nothing particularly dramatic had happened yet—and looked out at his audience.

"The name of this seminar is 'Taking Ownership.'" Another pause. "I wonder if anyone knows what I mean by that. It sounds a bit Draconian, I know. Taking ownership."

He raised his hands over his head and wiggled his fingers like a cartoon vampire preparing to strike.

"A bit like seizing power, isn't it, but what sort of power am I talking about? Or what kind of seizing? Well, I can assure you, your managers did not ask me to speak to you today so you could throw a lunchtime coup."

Laughter. I searched the crowd for Mary and finally found her toward the front, sitting between John Landsdale and Marge Boyton. Something bunched itself up in my chest. I felt betrayed.

"Ownership," he said. "To me that means being more than just a part of the team. A true team, a true team dynamic, functions not as individual parts, but as one thing. And if you are truly integrated into that thing, then you—in a very real sense—own it."

He paused again, nodding to himself, giving us all a chance to digest this bit of wisdom. John Landsdale leaned forward and whispered something into Mary's ear. She nodded enthusiastically.

"There is no place for 'ego' when you are an active owner of the team."

He made quotation marks in the air with his fingers.

"There is no place for 'competition'."

The same little gesture in the air.

"One who assists the team with ownership doesn't use force over his employees. Such a course will backfire. A good leader fulfills his purpose, nothing more or less than that. He doesn't use force or intimidation to seize power for himself. He fulfills his purpose, but isn't proud or boastful. He doesn't go around bragging. He fulfills his purpose because he has no other choice."

At that moment a curtain at the back of the stage opened to reveal a screen. The red-haired man turned to face it as it jumped forward with a sudden brightness. With a click, the blank light was replaced with the image of a man in a tuxedo and a woman in a white dress, both smiling out at the audience with yards and yards of glowing teeth and sparkling eyes. They were familiar to me, though not as clearly and as immediately as one might think, given the fact that I was the man and my wife was the woman. It took a moment to burn itself into my brain while I considered the possibility that they were just models—models that bore a striking resemblance to my widow and myself.

It was a picture from our wedding. My wife and I were standing at the front of the courtroom, before the judge with the broken finger. A few witnesses sat in the jury box.

"What makes a marriage work?" the man on the stage asked.

The slide then changed to a closer shot of my wife and me smiling at the camera.

"A marriage is a partnership, like any business, like any team. It is built on trust, mutual respect, selflessness, affection."

Next slide: rice being thrown as the newlyweds leave the courthouse, smiling, shielding their eyes from the sun and flying objects. I had some dim memory of being hit in the eye by one small grain of rice thrown by some overzealous clerk as my wife and I made our way to the car.

"It is a contract, much like the contract you share with the Komacor Corporation, much like the one you share with each and every member of your project team. A unity . . . a marriage of ideas, commitments, goals."

The next slide revealed the same picture, altered so it looked as if it had been torn in two, a jagged white-edged line dividing the man and woman.

"But what causes so many marriages to break up?" The speaker stared out at the audience as if waiting for an answer.

"Car wrecks," I muttered to myself.

"What was that?" the guy sitting next to me asked.

"She looks a lot like my wife," I said.

"Oh? She's very pretty."

"Thank you."

"Makes a lot of sense," he said nodding thoughtfully toward the stage.

"Hmm?"

"This guy. A lot of sense."

"Uh-huh," I said without much enthusiasm.

"Ego," the man on the stage said. "That's what destroys most marriages. Not money, or jealousy, or sexual problems. Putting oneself over the team. When one person is in charge of a marriage, there is no real marriage. You don't own your wife or husband. You own the marriage—the institution—the partnership . . . the team. And you own it by being a *part* of the team."

This seemed to be his final restatement and explanation of his point. A rather bland point, I thought. And a rather confused metaphor.

He was silent for a moment. Then the screen behind him went black. "Thank you for your time," he said, as he nodded solemnly to the audience and walked off the stage. There was a polite round of applause. Then the stage lights dimmed and I could hear the sound of things being pushed hurriedly across the floor, the squeak of rubber-soled shoes, and a few indistinct words muttered quietly.

Someone in the audience coughed and, as if it was the mating call of some bird or wild animal, the cough was answered on the opposite side of the auditorium in a slightly higher pitch.

The stage lights came on again, this time to reveal a table, chair, lamp, and behind them, the framework of a window and door. A man sat in the chair. Another man stood behind the couch. They were tall, slender and dark-haired, dressed in black suits, white shirts and black ties.

"The thing is," said the first actor (the one standing behind the couch) to the second, projecting his words loudly enough so that they could be heard in the back seats of the auditorium. "The thing is you were not there in the first place."

The second actor leaned forward, ran his hands through his hair, stood up and took several steps toward the edge of the stage.

"Oh? Oh? And where was I?" he bellowed.

"Somewhere else," said the first actor.

"Well I'm here now, aren't I? I'm here right now!"

I was struck by the notion that the last sentence was an ad lib, and I briefly imagined a scene in rehearsal with the actor explaining that the words needed the emphasis of repetition, the writer arguing that it was just redundancy and cheap dramatics, and the director giving in to the actor because it was just some crappy motivational skit and he didn't need to appease the writer anymore since the thing had already been written.

The first actor stood up, walked to the opposite edge of the stage, and, looking out into the audience (though with the stage lights shining up at him he probably saw only a dark void) said: "Now is too late."

The man next to me leaned over and whispered: "I'm not sure I get the point to this part."

"Me neither," I agreed. I wondered for a moment if this wasn't some other forgotten scene from my life, stolen from my past and put on display—like my wedding photos—as an example of bad teamwork and non-ownership.

"How can it be too late," the actor said. "I'm here now. We're together. We can work this out, can't we?"

"The order was due yesterday. What are you going to do, Superman? Fly around the globe at the speed of light and turn back time?"

"I don't think you're being very helpful."

"You left me out to dry."

"OK. OK. I heard you. I hear what you're saying . . ."

A third actor entered from stage left. He was dressed in a white suit and walked toward the two men in a bouncy gait that seemed designed to illustrate an upbeat, optimistic and all-around positive attitude.

"Tom! Bill!" he said, clapping the closest one to him on the shoulder. "I heard about the Hovel account. Let's put our heads together and see how we can resolve this! No point in assigning blame! This is the time for us to come together as a team!"

Spots began to float in front of my eyes. Blood-red spots with rims of green cilia. They swam and darted about, bumped into one another and threatened to mate. A sickly dampness crawled over my face. I quickly stood up and worked my way through the gauntlet of knees to the aisle. As I left the auditorium I could hear the actors droning on, their voices muddling as the door closed behind me, fading into an annoying memory as I went up the steps, left the lobby and walked out into what I had forgotten was a beautiful and sunny day.

I already knew there would be hell to pay the next day because of my sudden departure. John Landsdale would step into the area around my desk that used to be my office and say "We missed you yesterday." There would be an ominous tone dripping from his words. From across the room, Mary would smile a sympathetic smile toward me. And, Marge Boyton, off in the distance, past potted plants and the blur of activity, would stare blankly.

I walked home, feeling better in the sun, remembering the pictures on the screen that were from my life but that seemed more like stock photos used in a business seminar.

# -27-

How much time had gone by in that world that still clicked off time neatly? The sun still rose and set in an accelerated pattern. Clouds and shadows still skidded by in fast motion across the darkening, lightening, darkening sky. The movie my brother had watched in the theater was now playing on the TV in my sister's living room. The plot was well advanced. The man, the cut on his brow healed to a thin, dark scab, was chasing the mad bomber through an abandoned factory. Explosions went off around him, filling the air with debris and flower-like plumes of fire and smoke. The mad bomber looked down from on high, a small remote in his hand and a maniacal grin on his face as he pressed a red button and said with an evil giggle: "Kablam."

"And this day started out so well," the hero said, a fresh cut on his chin, a smudge of soot on his cheek.

~

# CLOUD 8

Robert slept in his bed, the night-light on. Even through the twisting clutter of sheets it was obvious he had grown. Taller and leaner, his face had lost some vital fraction of its cherubic nature and now bore the future ghost of what he would look like as a man.

~

Thomas sat in his apartment. The clutter had shifted around him. The colors and sizes of the papers on the floor may have changed, but the effect was the same: the same rubble of his life, the same symbol of his disorder. He was watching TV. His favorite show. The artist was getting married, not to the beautiful model that was his girlfriend, but to the beautiful woman who was his assistant and who was now played by a different and more noticeably buxom actress.

It was a lavish, outdoor wedding, with several classic types from the art world (the snobs, the flakes, the eccentrics, the brooding geniuses) clashing in quiet whispers and arch looks with several family characters (the sad mothers, the disapproving fathers, the jealous brothers and supportive sisters) occupying the other side of the grassy aisle.

A dark and handsome (also brooding) young priest spoke eloquently—an eloquence I have never witnessed from real-life priests—of love, marriage, and commitment.

"If anyone can give just cause why this man and woman should not be married . . ."

There was a tense pause. Eyes darted from face to face as the guests sat on the edge of their seats, and then . . .

The beautiful (jilted) model appeared. She was drunk, a fact made evident not only by her un-steadiness as she walked up the aisle, but also by the carefully disheveled appearance of her hair, the rumpled evening gown she has been wearing since last night, and the prop bottle of pink champagne clutched tightly in one hand.

"I know a reason! You bet your goddamn ass I know a reason."

The show broke for a commercial, and the ads were all for products I had never heard of, prod-ucts that would not have been advertised on TV during my lifetime: genital lubricants, vibrators, sexual stimulants. (One wonders of the show's tar-geted demographics.) Prolong-O, a cream that "en-hances pleasure for both hims and hers." (And oh what a clever man like myself could have done with an assignment like that: "Prolong-O . . . keep that 'haven't-finished-yet' luster." "Prolong-O . . . Good for a goose, good for a gander." "Prolong-O . . . it's not your father's hair-cream.")

~

# CLOUD 8

In a hotel room William undressed the blue-haired girl, clearly not for the first time. There was a confidence to the way he unzipped the side of her skirt, pulled the T-shirt over her head, unclasped her bra. There was no fear of rejection or overstepping bounds. He had been here before, had seen these soft treasures enough for them to lose their initial thrill of discovery, if not their over-all appeal. With an idle casualness she unbuttoned his shirt and kissed his chin.

My brother's hair was thinning. When he removed his shirt, I saw that he had gained both weight and body hair since the last time he and I swam together in that lake by the cottage my family used to rent for the summer.

"How long do you have?" she asked, laying naked across the sheets, her body all young soft curves, pale flesh, dark pink points, a rose tattoo on her ankle. The dark, wispy hair between her legs (it was not blue) had been carefully trimmed into the shape of a lightning bolt.

"How long do these work functions usually last?" William answered, and she giggled like a little girl until he covered her mouth with his own.

As he moved down to kiss her neck, she said: "Sometimes they go all night. Don't they? Can't they?"

His response was lost against the skin of her

shoulder. His hand moved between her legs, which opened to him. Gasp and murmur. Wet sounds. Things slipping in.

"Shit," my brother said suddenly.

"What?"

"Hold still. Don't move."

"What?"

"My ring came off."

"What? Where? Is it in the bed? Maybe it's in the bed?"

"It's not in the bed. Hold still."

"Holy shit!"

"Hold still. How far could it go?"

"Holy shit, are you kidding?"

"Hang on. Don't move."

Finally, my brother sat up triumphantly, holding up the golden band. It gleamed wetly in the hotel lamplight.

"Jesus," she said and laughed. "How far could it go? Have you heard of the birth canal, for Christ's sake?"

"I have some passing acquaintance with it, yes," he said, placing his wedding ring on the nightstand next to the lamp and a half-empty tube of Prolong-O.

~

I turned it off. It's not good to watch too

much TV. Or to sit directly in front of the screen. Hard lumps form in the center of your brain, like a pebble in a shoe, inflaming and infecting the soft tissue around it.

I went to bed and fell asleep to the water falling again in my box on the dresser, the voices coming through the melting walls, the footsteps walking on the ceiling above me.

I flew above the clouds.

# -28-

John Landsdale pressed his white-fleshed knuckles against the edge of my desk and looked at me for an uncomfortable moment before speaking.

"We missed you yesterday," he said.

"I was sick."

"Really? Not pinkeye again, I hope."

"No. Nausea. Dizziness. Flu-like symptoms. It came over me all of a sudden during the seminar. I went out for some fresh air, then just thought it would be better if I went home."

"You should have told someone before you left."

"I should have. You're right. It just came over me all of a sudden."

"I see."

He stayed there looking at me, and I wondered if his face was supposed to be stern, questioning, or disappointed. His eyes reminded me of melting ice cubes cracking in the bottom of some cloudy glass, snapping, crackling and popping as they fractured along strange interior lines.

"I'm here now," I said, becoming suddenly too irritated by his eyes, his knuckles and his silence to worry about how my words might sound. "I'm here right now."

He made a face, his bottom lip shortening, thinning, wrinkling up pink and bloodless, eyes narrowing, with one—just one—nostril flaring. Then he turned and walked away.

I expected him to stop at Mary's desk, to share with her their latest little private joke, but he only walked passed her nodding. He stopped at Marge Boyton's desk, leaning over to say something quietly into her ear. She looked back at me as his lips moved—staring across the desks and potted plants, her face a complete blank.

I glanced at Mary, or, more accurately, the top of Mary's head. She was looking down at the work on her desk—looking down, I thought, a little too studiously. Was she avoiding my stare? Had I become the doomed man that no one wanted to be near or look at directly?

I turned to my computer and tried to concentrate on my work, and after a few minutes or so managed to bury myself in the business of replacing, deleting, rearranging and renaming.

At the end of the day, I stopped by Bob Lenworth's office, tapping politely on his partially opened door. He looked up from his desk and smiled broadly, making the lines on his Abraham Lincoln face grow deep and shadowy.

"James!" he said, setting the stovepipe hat he held in his hand onto the desk and leaning back into his plush red-velvet theater chair. "I'm glad you stopped by. Come on in. Tell me how things are going down there."

"Well, that's why I wanted to see you, actually."

He gestured with one large hand toward the chair on the opposite side of the desk. I sat down.

"Yes?" he said.

"I was wondering if maybe you couldn't find me another position."

He raised one of his considerable set of eyebrows. "Oh? Are you unhappy down there?"

"I wouldn't say unhappy, exactly. I just don't think I'm getting the hang of it. I'm not sure it's right for me there. I was thinking maybe there might be a position I'm more suited for somewhere else."

"Hmm," he said.

"I guess I expected more from death."

He laughed. A big, booming, historical laugh. "That's very clever. I can see why you were in advertising. 'Expected more from death.' Very clever indeed."

"Yeah. I was pretty good in advertising. Isn't there anything . . . "

"I wish to heck we had an advertising department, Jim. I really do. You would be perfect."

"Maybe I could start one," I said hopefully. He smiled the kind of smile people give you when they want you to know that they like your idea, they're glad that you thought of it, and they find it completely without merit.

"We don't need one, Jim. If we did . . ."

"I'd be perfect for it."

"Exactly."

"I see." I tried not to pout.

"Give it some more time up there, Jim. You'll get comfortable with things. By all reports you're doing a great job."

I leaned forward. "I find that hard to believe."

"I could show them to you." He glanced at a file cabinet, as if that's where the reports were stored, but made no move to retrieve them. Instead he paraphrased: "Hard worker, conscientious, good eye for details, that sort of thing."

"I'd *like* to see them."

"Well, I can't *really* show them to you. I just meant, they're there. They exist. You'll just have to take my word for it."

"Oh."

He stood and picked up his hat. He didn't put it on his head, but I got the idea clearly enough. I got up and went to the door.

"Well, thanks for your time anyway," I told him while he smiled and nodded down at me. He was, of course, a tall man.

"Give it time, Jim," he said. "Just give it some more time. You'll see. You can't force these things. Just fulfill your purpose on the team. That's all. Nothing more or less than that."

I stared at him for a moment as I stood in the doorway. "You were at that seminar too, huh?"

"It was mandatory, Jim."

# -29-

The couple next door was fighting loudly enough to be heard above the TV, where William and Maggie were also fighting. I turned the volume down and watched as my brother and his wife acted out the neighbors' argument, their lips not matching exactly, but the flushed faces, knitted brows, pointless kicking movements at air, folded arms and clenched fists that went nowhere approximating almost perfectly the heated words of my neighbors.

"Do you think I'm a fool?" the woman said as Maggie mouthed some similar sentence. "You must think I'm a complete idiot!"

And while my brother held his hands limply at his side, then suddenly raised them to make a point, then lowered them again as the point evaporated, there was silence next door. When my brother finally opened his mouth, the man next door said: "I don't think you're an idiot. But just because you feel something is so, it doesn't make it so.

Everything that pops into your head is not instantly a fact, you know."

"Every other night!" the woman shouted, though in this instance Maggie only appeared to mutter the same words. "How can I not start to 'feel' something? How is the obvious supposed to not pop into my head?"

"But look," the man said, as William again raised his hands in some version of a reasoning gesture. "Just because you feel that way . . . Just because . . . So I work late some nights. So I haven't been here as much as I used to. It doesn't stand to reason from that . . . "

"I called for you at work, you should know. Before you go on being so reasonable."

William's hands again died in the air and fell back to his sides, like little tangled knots at the ends of limp ropes. There was silence. When I heard the man's voice again, it contained a controlled note of fury, righteous anger and hurt. Backed into a corner, perhaps, he had put on the mask of the wronged man. Or perhaps, unlike my brother, he was truly innocent.

"And? And what did they say? That I was out in some sleazy hotel room cheating on you, but you could leave a message if you wanted?"

"They didn't say anything. There was no one there."

"Well, there you go. Obviously I was up to something. Obviously I was up to no good." My brother ran his hands through his thinning hair. "Did it ever occur to you that now and then, just possibly, work gets done away from the office? Does the phrase 'business dinner' mean anything at all to you?"

"Don't talk to me like I'm an idiot. I'm not an idiot, so don't talk to me like I am."

Were there tears in my sister-in-law's eyes? Was there a sob in my neighbor's voice? William's face softened, if not in defeat, then at least in some form of regret.

"Look," the man said as my brother stepped closer to his wife. "I'm not cheating on you. I love you. OK?"

Maggie looked at him, but did not step into his open arms. "I love you too," the woman said. "But I can't go on like this. Not trusting you. Not knowing what to believe."

"Then trust me," he said. "Believe in me."

"How can I?"

"Why can't you?"

"Where were you then?"

"I was having drinks with a client. It's that kind of business, honey. I have to coddle them, but believe me, I don't do it with any great passion. I only kiss them on the cheek. Like the Mafia."

They were quiet next door after that. I turned off the TV and went to bed. I thought of a fellow I worked with once at the advertising firm who wrote novels and stories on the side. I don't know if they were any good—I had successfully managed to avoid ever reading one of them. But he once told me something that stuck with me. He said: the trick to happy endings is knowing when to stop talking.

I didn't watch TV again for some time after that.

Drifting off into sleep that night, as the gold, yellow, blue and green lights of the falls slid over everything, I noticed a crack in the ceiling. I was sure it had not been there before. What had caused it? It seemed to be shaped like some kind of animal or something. A rabbit? There might have been an ear and an incomplete amount of whiskers. A dog? A dog chasing a ball? Or maybe a child? A child chasing a ball? Or possibly a dog chasing a child chasing a ball chasing a rabbit? Before I could figure it all out, I was asleep, skimming across the tops of clouds, clouds that were shaped like rabbits, dogs and children.

# -30-

The late afternoon light stretched itself along the office floor, crawling up the sides of desks, laying itself out across their tops, sparkling and rippling within water bottles and glittering against the elemental flecks in Mary's hair.

The light, even this waning light, seemed to push against John Landsdale like a measurable force—like a wind or tide. He reached the edge of my desk and rested.

I waited patiently to hear what new area of my work performance was deficient.

Finally, he said: "I'm having a little get-together after work tonight. You're welcome to come if you can make it."

There was something in the way he worded the invitation that seemed designed to give me a way out, but I smiled up at him (not a warm smile, exactly) and answered: "Sounds great. I'll be there with bells on."

He nodded, showing the yellow, almost

translucent teeth in his mouth, then turned and walked away. I glanced at Mary, sitting at her desk, watching with a look on her face that was not quite curious enough. I knew immediately that John Landsdale was only acting on her suggestion. I pictured her making it one evening over drinks: Oh, that James Broadhurst is a nice enough fellow, when you get to know him. Invite him to your party. He might be hurt if you don't.

I nodded at her and she smiled, revealing her one slightly crooked tooth. Did she pity me, or did she sincerely desire my presence at this little get-together? Should I have felt grateful or resentful?

~

There was no bell that rang, no whistle that blew to signify the end of the workday at the Komacor Corporation. Your days were killed gradually by a feeling of either accomplishment or futility. It was a slow and semi-natural death. You watched your fellow workers across slabs of brassy light and bided your time, waiting for a sign that the day was ending—the turning off of computers, the putting away of mysterious papers into locked drawers, the casual stroll to the community sink to wash out today's brown coffee cup stains. And then, one by one, you left.

# CLOUD 8

Outside the building, I caught a blue cab that took me to a white house on top of a green hill. Dreading this party a little, I had let everyone in the office leave before me for the first time since I had joined the Komacor family.

I stepped from the cab as soft party sounds—the clink of glasses, the murmur of voices, small and scattered explosions of laughter—rolled across the lawn through the growing darkness.

I traveled without hurry up a stone walkway that refused to go in a straight line, though a straight line could easily have been arranged. No trees or boulders stood in the way—the path was bordered only with small shrubs that were cut, carved, or otherwise manipulated into the shapes of animals. A swan. A horse. A dinosaur.

I reached the house and knocked unenthusiastically on the front door. The door opened under the force of my knock, and there before me was the bright revelry of a John Landsdale party.

Parties, for me, have always been more enjoyable in legend than in fact. If a man at the water cooler spun his tale of debauchery from the night before, I would listen eagerly as vivid pictures filled my mind. I would hear the uncontrolled laughter and see the night spinning out in bright flashes of riotous scenes. If I read in a book about the all-night affairs at some city penthouse or country cottage, I could imagine clearly enough the golden light, the handsome, pretty people. But faced with the actuality of leaving the comfort of my own couch and TV and entering the alien environs of festivity, I saw only a forbidding, foreboding sea of elbows and faces, the dull and ordinary light that comes from sixty-watt bulbs, and the strained expressions as everyone searched awkwardly for a suitable topic of conversation while they waited for the alcohol to take effect.

Through the sea of elbows and faces, my boss, my host, John Landsdale, spied me by the door.

"James!" he said in a jovial voice that seemed to have been put on for the occasion like a black velvet smoking jacket. "Glad you could make it."

He did not push his way through his guests to meet me—and just as well, I thought, for a man who seemed to have to fight against the currents of sunlight and spring breezes. I made my way forward, past John Landsdale and the people he was talking with, across a thick blue carpet that sucked at my feet like mud, to a small bar set up on a rented table at the far side of the living room. Abraham Lincoln stood behind the table, smiling blandly at the party he served but was not a part of.

He fixed me a drink.

"Hey, you're not the head of human re-sources are you?" I asked him as an afterthought.

"No, sir."

"Didn't think so."

Beyond the wriggling mass of nodding heads, shifting feet and protruding elbows, I found a corner of relative quiet next to a potted fern and drank my drink quickly (and then another, and another), anxious for the softening effect of alcohol. It came in time, transforming the mass first into something pitiable, then something touching, and finally—if only temporarily—into a warm and affectionate sampling of humanity. A cheery bunch who loved each other equally and with complete sincerity. Women—pretty women—touched the arms of handsome men as they talked. Faces—such attractive faces—leaned in close, not in preparation or yearning for kisses, but to hear the sing-song of words and laughter that much sooner as they left pretty parted lips, carried lightly on the breeze of fruit-scented breath.

I stood at the outer edge of it all, chatting briefly with three or four friendly members of the Komacor family who ventured past, winded and laughing, as if thrown from the circle of some happy, energetic children's game (crack the whip, red rover red rover). They were only passing by, resting for a moment by me and my fern. They would say a word or two or four—"James! How you doing?"—or five—"James! Good to see you!"—then catch their breath, freshen their drinks and dive back in.

Eventually I left my corner and approached a cluster of people that seemed approachable, angling my way politely into their conversation, their children's game, their passing moment of cohesive affection and fleeting familial love.

". . . or move the release date back," a man (lantern-jawed, golden skinned) was saying. And then laughter. A woman (young and pretty) stood next to him, leaning against his broad shoulder as she giggled, spilling a bit of her pink-colored drink down the front of her white shirt.

"Oh jeez!" she said, still laughing as she tried to brush it off with her hand. A thin pink smear was left behind.

"Club soda," someone said.

"Or a new blouse."

"Club soda and a new blouse."

"Scotch and Soda and a new blouse."

More laughter.

"Want me to get you a paper towel?" I asked her.

She smiled. "No. I've got a million shirts just like this. I buy them by the dozen. Without the stains of course. I like to do that part myself."

"Such a talented girl," said the lantern-jawed man. The life of the party. The life of the afterlife.

But there was no way into their circle of merriment; its edges had already hardened into a protective shell. The laughs that they laughed were not really about the most recent funny thing said, but a culmination of all of the evening's witty remarks and good feelings. Their jokes were lost on me, as was their warmth.

Where was Mary?

I found her in another room, standing in front of a large-screen TV. Her face was lit beautifully, as if by sunlight.

The other people in the room were mostly unfamiliar to me: a young man touching the soft, black bangs of a woman on the couch, and another man—older and alone—leaning against a windowsill swirling the ice in his otherwise empty glass as a full, dime-sized moon rose above his left shoulder.

Steven Roth stood next to Mary, leaning forward to speak into her ear. She shook her head and smiled—always smiling, my Mary—then saw me standing in the entranceway.

"James!" she said. I walked over, smiling at Mary, nodding to Steven.

"What's the show?" I asked, waving my

drink toward the glowing screen.

"That's John's wife," she said. On the screen, a woman with large waves of yellow hair was sitting at a dining room table. At the other end of the table a dark man with a thin mustache was struggling with the cork of a bottle of wine.

"John Landsdale's married?" I asked.

"Well, till death do us part and all that," Steven Roth laughed. "So you tell me. Is that license expired?"

John Landsdale entered the room, a drink in his hand. There was a rosy, unfamiliar color in his cheeks and a bright dampness to his eyes. His party face. Or his face after drinking.

"Hey John," Steven said. "Who's the guy with your wife?"

John Landsdale sneered, and his teeth shone like white tombstones, glistening with spit and drink. There was a solidity to them, a solidity which never showed at work.

"Her husband," he said. "My former business partner."

"Ouch."

John Landsdale shrugged. Mary said: "Oh John," and touched the sleeve of his jacket. I sipped my drink and said nothing.

On TV, the man finally got the cork out of the bottle.

# CLOUD 8

"It gave me quite a fight," he said laughing.

John Landsdale, his tongue sounding thick in his mouth, said: "I always wondered about him and my wife. Never trusted the bitch."

He glanced nervously at Mary, to see, I suppose, if he had offended her. Nothing changed in her face. It was as soft, open and polite as always.

"Ah well." He forced a smile. "It was never what you would have called a perfect marriage. It lacked . . ." His eyes looked up, in search of the word.

"Passion?" I offered.

His eyes came down again as if from a long ways away. "Yes. Passion. In a word. Thank you, James. Always a good man with the word, eh?"

"I only say because my own wife . . ." I began, but did not feel like finishing.

John Landsdale was indeed a different man drunk. A solid man with blood that showed beneath his skin, words that forced themselves loudly, if in somewhat mangled condition, and a walk (I witnessed it as Mary followed him out of the room) propelled forth with an energy that he did not possess sober. A controlled cowboy stumble moving forward.

"Marriage is sacrifice," Steven said, raising his glass toward the TV in a toast. "Human sacrifice."

Mary turned off the TV.

"I hate parties where the TV is always on. It just kills the mood. Everyone ends up sitting on the couch just staring."

"Right you are, Mary," John Landsdale said, as he casually slipped his arm around her waist. "Right you are. No more TV! I banish TV from the kingdom!" Then the two of them disappeared together into an unfriendly and unbreakable carapace of men and women, suits and cocktail dresses, and bottomless cups.

The fact that alcohol seemed to make John Landsdale the opposite of what he was during the day made me as distrustful of his phantom self as I was currently annoyed by this boisterous and bitter one. It struck me that there was something fraudulent at the core of him. Or maybe I only resented his arm around that soft, narrow waist that I so clearly wanted my own arms around.

Steven reached past me and turned the TV back on.

"I defile the order of the king," he said.

"Defy, you mean."

"Always a quick man with the right word, eh James?"

But there was only static on the screen now.

~

Later and drunker, I saw Bob Lenworth standing in a small crowd of faceless people by a bay window.

"Hey, I mistook the bartender for you," I told him.

He laughed and said: "But I go for the more traditional look." He touched the top of his stove-pipe hat.

"Oh, I know. But just for a moment I thought . . ."

"Hoof and mouth!" a man near us said loudly—not to Bob Lenworth or me, but to whatever particular sub-group he was entertaining.

"Mad cow!" someone shouted back to the accompaniment of much laughter.

Someone else: "Not at these low prices!"

Someone else: "Only word that parrot knows!"

Much much laughter.

"You sure you're not the bartender?" I asked Bob Lenworth.

"Across the room," he said. "Fellow without the hat."

~

Much later and much drunker, I saw Mary by the bar.

"Hey," I said. "Are you and John Landsdale

an item or something?"

"An item?" she laughed.

"An item."

"What's an item?"

"An item."

She smiled, but it was a smile that meant nothing, or at least, told me nothing. Red-brown lips with no teeth showing. Where was John Landsdale? Somewhere nearby I was sure. Sauntering his way back to Mary.

"I don't know what you mean," she said. "An item."

"Clearly."

She frowned, which also seemed to mean nothing—or I was no longer capable of reading these things, drunk as I was. I suddenly felt guilty.

"That may have come off a little more bitter than I intended," I said.

"Clearly."

"Sorry."

"No harm."

She made a small, indecipherable shrug and walked away, leaving me standing there, swaying slightly and wondering what had happened, what was happening and what would happen next.

Why did I care? Why did I want her? Was it really even her, or just the limitation of choices in this life after life? She may only have been the most interesting fish in a dull pond, but I knew that the pond might be eternal, and how could I not grasp at something soft in the face of that?

Still later, I threw up in John Landsdale's bathroom. It was a nice bathroom, with dark green walls and a preponderance of golden fixtures and white ceramic handles. It took me some time, much toilet paper and a few guest towels to remove the evidence of my violent crime. It had splattered even to his gold-framed full-length mirror.

There was a tube of Prolong-O in his medicine cabinet.

~

I left the bathroom, house and party unnoticed and stood for a moment in the green darkness of the front lawn, gazing up at the glowing white house that clinked and laughed and leaked golden light from all its windows. Then I started home.

The sky grew black as I walked, and my drunkenness faded. My brain and eyes became clear again as I traveled down dark sidewalks, past houses, trees, street lamps, fire hydrants, bus stops, apartments, stores, skyscrapers, and bars. A passing bus let off a small explosion from its tailpipe, belching smoke that stank of burned oil and rust.

Reaching my building, I found a light burned out in the lobby and another one out above the stairs.

I undressed wearily, put on my pajamas, and plugged in the night-light. The couple next door was talking quietly, their voices cottony abstractions brushing softly against the walls. They were in love again, I imagined. The man had learned his lessons and all was right again in their version of the world.

I stared up at the crack in the ceiling—a ball chasing a rabbit chasing a child, or a child throwing a ball at a rabbit, or a rabbit tossing a child in the air like a ball. Soon I was far above it, far enough to see the world's round shape, the swirling vaporous cogs of cloud and water and the solid brown, green and gray clumps of the continents. I circled the globe and saw the soft line between day and night, and the twinkling star-like lights of neighborhoods and cities forming their irregular grids and then . . . BANG!

A loud sound awakened me, and though I opened my eyes to darkness and the same cracked ceiling and the same watery light, the noise seemed to vibrate in the air like a visible force radiating outwards in rippling circles overhead.

Is it too dramatic to say that I leapt from my bed? That I ran without thinking, still in my pajamas, out of the apartment and up the stairs? That I was knocking urgently at the door before I even realized that I had thrown off my covers?

Would it be too much for me to tell you that it was an angel that answered the door? But that's what it was. An angel with red hair that fell in tiny waves across the pink white roundness of her bare shoulders. She held a white bedsheet with one hand to her chest, and the sheet flowed down her body in a network of rolling folds and shadows.

But I do not call her an angel because of that—or because she was beautiful, with red Cupid's bow lips, almond-shaped eyes, and gentle fleshy curves that pushed and peeked from behind her sheet. No, I say she was an angel because she had wings—literal wings with small white feathers that sprouted from some point in the upper part of her back, rising up behind her like a second pair of shoulders so that one could imagine for a moment that some little bright white and downy man or child was standing on a step stool behind her with his back against hers and his head sagging out of sight down upon his chest.

"I heard a noise," I said as she stared at me with a bemused look that seemed more curious than hostile.

"I was dancing," she said.

"Dancing?"

"And I fell. You must have heard me fall."

"Yes. I guess that's what I heard. Are you

all right?"

"I like to dance but I'm not very good at it. I tend to fall."

She bowed suddenly and gracelessly. I had to step back to keep her head from crashing against me.

"I don't know. I think I have a bump. Right here. Feel." She pointed to a spot at the base of her skull, pulling her hair aside and spreading her wings. Stretched out to their full length they reached half an arm's-length out on either side before tapering off into thin points.

I touched her head lightly: a small hard knot had risen from the bone of her skull.

"Ugh," she said.

"You have a bump," I told her. "Maybe you should put some ice on it."

"I should. I should. Excellent idea." She turned and walked to the kitchen, leaving me in the doorway watching the smooth shifting lines of her as she walked. The sheet scooped low and loose to the small of her back, yet managed somehow to stay securely wrapped at the waist, allowing her hips to move in a pleasant rhythm beneath. One corner of the sheet trailed behind her on the floor, and looked, by its frayed edges and general dinginess, as if it had been dragging behind her for some time. Her wings stirred a little, like two absent-minded flaps, as she disappeared into the kitchen.

"Have you any ice?" I heard her call out from behind the freezer door. "I seem to have drunk all mine."

"Yes," I said. "Downstairs. I'll go get some . . ."

"Never mind. I have something." She came back a moment later holding a package of frozen peas against the back of her head. "Normally I don't even like vegetables," she said with a small and musical giggle.

I took a step into the room. It was an apartment like mine—same size and layout, same darkly varnished and uneven floors, same beige walls—but there was no furniture in it at all except for a green, threadbare couch that stood in the middle of the living room. There was no coffee table, no TV. Just the one couch, like a green island surrounded by a dull brown sea, and on the floor next to it a half-empty bottle and a completely empty glass.

"Close the door after yourself, kind neighbor, and have a drink with me," she said, dropping down, sheet, wings and all, into the center of the couch. If it had been daylight—with sunlight streaming through her unadorned windows—I feel certain that dust would have risen from the couch cushions in a thin cloud that would have curled up in the swirling air currents at her feathery tips. As it was, I could smell it in the air and taste it on my lips. It burned against the bare bulb overhead. The bulb in my apartment had a covering.

"Sit. Sit," she said.

I sat at the far end of the sofa. The tip of her wing brushed against my ear. She smiled apologetically and pulled them back in close.

"But I only have one glass left, I'm afraid. Do you mind sharing?"

"I don't mind."

"I have no cooties," she laughed.

"Me neither," I said, in lieu of something clever.

She filled the glass (a large one) and took the first sip. She made a face, her nose wrinkling up at its pointy tip as her mouth became small and lipless for a moment. Then she smiled broadly, showing her yellow-white teeth. Above them her eyes sparkled, but not too brightly.

"Can you tell that I'm drunk?"

"I could tell that you fell. Are you an angel?"

"Because I fell?"

"Because you have wings."

"Oh anyone can have wings. You just have to ask for them."

"Who?"

"Anyone who wants them."

"I mean who do you have to ask?"

She smiled, looked down at herself and adjusted the sheet slightly without any great concern for modesty.

"The guy who gives out wings. I forget his name. Tall guy, as I recall. In black. After that it's all a haze. Quite a day, that was. Big events. Lots happening. But I remember he was tall and in black. And I said, where are my wings, and he said, they're on your back. I don't know how I missed them. Then there was a lot of business about cab rides and post offices. I can't fly, you know. They are non-functional wings. I was very disappointed when I found that out."

"Near luggage claim?"

She looked at me.

"This guy who gave out the wings."

She handed me the glass and I took a sip.

"You had luggage?" she asked, but even as she asked, her eyes—green eyes, golden brown at the edges—seemed to move inward to some bright spot in her brain, to some other question that led to another question that led to an amusing fact that caused her to smile suddenly and then giggle.

She was not, strictly speaking, beautiful. There was a blemish or two on the pale, almost sickly skin of her face. Her bottom lip was decidedly thicker than her top one, giving her face a slightly petulant look, even when she smiled. Her nose was narrow, bent slightly at the bridge and almost disconcertingly sharp at the point. Her hair was a bit of a mess. But she was an angel nonetheless, with a radiance that was beyond healthy skin and perfect features.

"I had luggage," I told her, even though I knew she was no longer waiting for an answer.

"Should I get dressed?" she asked.

"If you want."

"I don't want. I like to walk around in a sheet. I think it goes nicely with the wings, don't you? Besides which, it is a pain in the ass to find pajamas that can accommodate these monstrosities." She flapped her wings twice, for emphasis.

I nodded and took another sip, feeling the warm, pleasant line the booze made from mouth to stomach.

"Clothes are a bore, but I want to be a good hostess. You're the first neighbor I've had over."

"You're the first neighbor I've visited."

"And all thanks to a bump of the head to the floor."

She stopped, thought for a second, then reworded her statement: "All thanks to my head bumping your ceiling."

She took the glass from my hand and raised it in a toast.

"Here's to clumsiness."

She took a long swallow that diminished the drink by a third.

"Should I say something about new beginnings? I should probably say something about new beginnings."

"It's my turn though," I said, taking the glass and raising it. "To new beginnings." I took a drink, almost as big as hers. The liquor burned my throat and made my eyes water. I smiled at her with wet and, I imagine, unsteady lips, and said, "Smooth."

She turned the corners of her lips downward and said: "I see why I didn't say it.    It sounds so corny.  New beginnings.  Sheesh."

"Maybe.  But still . . ." I had run out of anything else to say and wanted to kiss her now.  I wanted to lean forward right then and kiss her as if this were nothing more than a dream, with the spontaneity of a dream, the lack of consequences of a dream, the impermanence of a dream.

She yawned and I could not tell if it was a real yawn or a clue.

I said: "Well . . . I suppose I ought to let you go to bed," hoping that she would argue.  But she only smiled sweetly, her eyes blinking three times.

She followed me to the door.

"Thank you for coming to my rescue," she said.  I turned.  She was the same height as me, her face close to mine as I lingered for a moment.

"Maybe we could do something sometime," I said, rather lamely.

"How could we not?" she asked, but she was already stepping back, closing the door. The last thing I saw before it shut was one slanting, green-gold eye, her long narrow nose, half her smiling, pouting mouth, and a flash of red hair.

# -31-

I didn't go into work the next day. Lying in bed long past when I knew I should be up, I felt the sunlight pressing heavily against my blankets, like a thing that had weight. Stronger, warmer, brighter, heavier it became until finally I kicked the blankets off, got up, dressed and left the apartment.

I walked for something like miles opposite the direction I usually took to the Komacor Corporation, thinking about the angel, Mary, Pamela, my nebulous wife, my father and the rest of my family. I also thought about wings, and remembered the cardboard ones my mother would cut from boxes for Susan and me when we were kids. We would strap them to our arms with rubber bands or twine, then run flapping around the house and backyard, leaping from the second or third step of the porch, imagining that we were flying, and that the wings were slowing—in some discernable way—our inevitable fall to earth.

A taxicab drove by, its wheel wells dark and

jagged with rust, the red of the rust bubbling like a scab along the edges of bite-shaped wounds.

I passed a park and, realizing that I had not passed many parks in this city, I walked through its black iron gates (the word "PARK" was spelled out above in wrought iron leaves and branches) and entered a small, organized forest of young trees and green grass. A cobblestone path wound through it, and every hundred yards or so a green wooden bench waited empty and inviting. I sat down on one, leaned back in the sun, closed my eyes, and watched the red glowing blotches on the insides of my eyelids dart and bounce like playful one-celled organisms. Through the flutter of leaves in the wind, I could just make out the sound of the traffic going by outside the park: the whine and cough of taxi-cabs, the groans and backfires of buses. They were struggling, it seemed to me, struggling to move forward, laboring at the slightest incline or bump. At one time they had all seemed so well-oiled and new.

The dancing blobs of sunlight that played on the inside of my eyelids reminded me for some reason of children in a park, and it slowly occurred to me that if this afterlife were a movie, the hero would at this moment survey the city, his lantern jaw thrust out, his steel-blue eyes squinting in concern, and say to the mini-skirted heroine at his side:

"Don't you see what's wrong?"

She would look around, her face growing concerned, as a device hanging like a purse at her side began to beep urgently. She would take the device into her hand and begin to scan the grass and trees. The device would beep wildly, then hum. She'd pause, her eyes wide open in surprise, her mouth formed in the shape of the letter o, to reveal to the hero her shocking findings.

"No children," she'd say in the raspy whisper of unbelievable concern. "There are no children here!"

"Exactly," the hero would say, rubbing his considerable chin.

The blotches grew darker. The sun was going down, or slipping behind an impenetrable wall of clouds. I opened my eyes, stood up and walked back home.

~

Passing my own apartment on the stairs, I went one flight up to the apartment above. I knocked lightly at the door, thinking that maybe she was asleep, but the door opened and there she was with no sign of anything having changed from the night before. She still wore a bedsheet, her hair was still a pretty mess around her pale face, and she still smelled of last night's drinks.

"Did I fall again?" she asked.

"Just checking to see how your head is."

Her head was fine. She invited me in and again we sat on the couch, drinking from a brand new bottle, but from the same unwashed glass.

"Here's mud in your eye," she would say before knocking back a mouthful. Or: "Here's how," or "To all the fine young ladies and gentlemen." I made my own toasts as well ("Here's looking at you," "Here's to your mother," "Here's mud in your throat"). The evening slid into night. We talked and laughed about many things, most of which I cannot clearly remember. I have only the dim recall of the outline of events without their substance, and the distinct but unnamable emotions that accompanied them.

I do remember that at some point she said something about missing moons that were not always full. As she said it, there was some new sparkle to her eyes, and her lips drew me towards them.

I leaned forward and kissed her, knowing that I wanted to and knowing that I could. Her lips were burning with the contents of our shared glass; her mouth opening into mine was soft and moving. It was the kiss that I had dreamt about countless times when I had been alive, but never actually experienced in life, as there had always been at least one eye that would pry itself open to look out at the face before me—made blurry by its closeness—and glance at the clock on the wall, the TV, or the world outside the window.

The kisses of women I had loved, the women I had not loved but had kissed anyway, my wife; I did not remember their mouths this way. What are the mechanics that makes one kiss special and another ordinary when it is all only lips and tongue and the soft touch of teeth?

Time passed smoothly, drunkenly and imperceptibly, freezing into one perfect moment unspoiled by past or future, by rust or decay. A beautiful insect trapped in amber, and all its happiness and contentment trapped with it. I opened one eye and saw her looking back with both.

She laughed into my mouth, pulled her face back and laughed louder. She then took a long drink from the glass that she had somehow kept from spilling while we kissed. Then she grabbed the bottle from the floor and refilled the glass. While she was doing this, the sheet slipped (finally) from one breast, revealing something small, round and soft, with a dark pink and pointed tip. Something perfect, I might say, but maybe I see too many things as perfect, which is perhaps a failing of mine, a lack of imagination or discrimination that causes me to cry beauty in a world that is not inherently beautiful.

My eyes jerked away in embarrassment.

She looked down, smiled and pulled the sheet back into place. I leaned forward again for another kiss, but she moved her face out of reach. The tip of her right wing slapped playfully at my chin.

"I should get some sleep," she said. "I am way too drunk. I will go straight to bed and refrain from dancing."

But her voice was clear; there was no thickness to any of her words or half-lidded dullness to her eyes.

I stood up, and doing so, felt my own drunkenness hit me with force.

"OK," I said, swaying. "I will leave you to your rest, then. I hope I will see you again soon. I hope our paths will cross again soon. I hope . . . that soon . . ."

"Of course you do. Of course they will."

I exited the room a yellow bouncing blur, the angel a pink and white one, dancing me to the doorway.

"Goodnight," she said. "And tomorrow perhaps we will find out each others' names."

"Yes," I said, realizing only then that we had not. "Yes, yes. We must, yes. I'm James . . ."

The door closed softly behind me.

# -32-

The next day I skipped work again, washing away whatever residual guilt I had with several cups of coffee.  Then I went out for my customary aimless walk.

The streets and sidewalks were nearly empty. A bus went by with a rumble and a sputtering cough.  A man stinking of beery piss and sweat shuffled by, his eyes fixed to the ground.  At a corner, a garbage can had been turned over, and its contents blew all over the street.

I saw a neon cocktail glass at another corner, and headed toward it.

The bar was uninhabited save for the bartender and my old friend Tom.

"Hi Tom," I said, taking the stool next to him.

He smirked his hello and asked: "No work today?"

"Playing hooky," I told him.  He nodded.  I did not ask him what he was doing there at this time of day himself. If he had lost another job I did not want to remind him of it, or hear him tell the sorry tale. There were gray bags beneath his red-rimmed eyes. The bottom half of his face was blue with a growth of short, sharp hairs. He could have been sitting there for days.

The bartender brought me a drink.

"This place is falling apart," Tom said thickly.

"The bar?"

"The city."

I glanced around the bar at first, and saw nothing out of the ordinary. But I thought about the city, and it's thinning traffic, littered streets, and shabby men. "I think maybe you're right," I said.

"I'll tell you why." He turned to face me. His fetid breath smelled like gasoline, and his body reeked of some undefinable order that reminded me of fermented flowers. He put a cigarette between his lips and lit it. It could only help.

"No pride," he said, then leaned back, as if to get out of the way of my expected enthusiasm for his having hit the nail so precisely on its elusive head.

"No pride, huh?" I said.

"No pride. No pride. Nobody has any pride anymore. Everything is falling apart 'cause nobody gives a shit 'cause nobody has any pride. Plenty of jobs, but no fucking pride. That's why everything is falling apart. That's why."

"I thought pride cameth before the downfall. Or something like that."

"Bullshit. I've seen it happen before, you know. Cities like this. You know how you can tell when a city is going down fast?"

"No," I said, but took a guess: "Litter in the streets? Rusting cars?"

"Wigs," he said.

"Wings?" I replied. I was now interested in what he had to say. What could Tom know of wings and their possible connection to the city's decline? I wondered if this was at last the defining and climactic moment in which not only life but also the afterlife would be explained to me? Was Tom, finally, my drunken Virgil? Would the great truths of the universe be delivered in a cloud of warm foul breath and cigarette smoke?

"Wigs," he said. "W . . . W-I . . . W-I-G."

Now I was just confused. "Wigs?"

"Wigs. Christ. Wigs, already."

"OK."

The bartender poured me another drink. Tom went on.

"When wig shops move in. Something about wig shops. A city starts dying and suddenly there's a wig shop at every corner. 24-hour wig shops.

Carry-out or delivery. Wigs-R-Us. We are wigs. Everyone needs a wig."

"If people don't have pride anymore, why would they need wigs?"

He stared at me. My point, which I thought valid enough, seemed to annoy him. He took a long, hard swallow from his glass and slammed it, empty, onto the bar.

"Another," he said to the bartender, who hesitated for a moment before refilling the glass.

I thought perhaps the subject of dying cities, pride, and wig shops had been given up, but a few moments later Tom said: "Wigs have nothing to do with pride."

I let it go. "OK."

"You don't believe me?"

"I believe you."

"Bullshit."

I didn't say anything. I drank my drink. Tom's lips moved silently and his eyes searched upward, as if he was praying or working a math problem out in his head. A prayer or a fifteen percent tip. But what was fifteen percent of nothing? Some amount of time passed that way.

"Wigs," Tom said again. "Wigs . . ." I could tell he was reaching for something. "Wigs . . . are a symptom. Wig shops . . . Anyway, who said people are buying wigs anyway? It's just that the shops

are there.  You never see customers.  And why?
Huh?    Why is that?"

I took a not-so-wild guess: "Because nobody
has any pride anymore?"

"Exactly!"  He narrowed his eyes at me, examining my face for sincerity.    "Goddamn exactly
right.  Whether you believe it or not."

~

On the way home the streets seemed even
more deserted, as litter and garbage blew in the
wind like symbolic tumbleweeds.  I passed a house
with boarded-up windows, a lawn overgrown with
weeds and grass gone to seed, and at every corner
it seemed as if wig shops were crouching in the shadows waiting to move in.

~

On the other side of my apartment's thin
walls, the fighting couple was silent.  I imagined
their life had returned to normal, to a new and better state of blissful happiness and reconfirmed love.
I imagined that the blue-haired girl who had almost
come between them was now going on with her own
young life, making this or that mistake again and
again, but finally learning, finally finding a free and
clear love of her own, and settling down in some
comfortable house in the country.  Maybe she had

dyed her hair blonde and the man at work had stopped loving her. But all this was a fantasy, and it made me sad, frustrated and nauseous. What was the point in imagining the happy endings of other people? Why worry or even think about characters who were nothing more than unclear and unseen voices through a wall? I had a wife once, and lost her through no fault of my own, but that was only a matter of timing. If I had lived, some fault of my own would have accomplished the act as well as any careless driver. I would have lost her, as I have lost her now, gone from life, memory and TV. I can say that I had a wife, but I cannot describe her to you now, or tell you any more stories, happy or sad, from my marriage. And I can imagine that divorce—if it had been a divorce rather than a car accident—is something like the lingering death of a loved one. Like my mother's death. When the slow, drawn out process is finally over, there is more relief than sorrow. You think only of the sickly smell of the dying, the bloating or withering of flesh, the muscles sagging loosely and ineffectively from the bone. And you forget, once it is gone, that before that slow rot there had once been a life that was full of life. But I had loved my mother, and had learned in time to miss her once again. And I loved my wife once; I know that I must have. And I know that there were days that, if I could now recall them clearly, would make me sorry she was gone.

It was night, and I went to sleep.

# -33-

In the morning I turned on the TV for the first time in I didn't know how long. A young man I did not immediately recognize stood in the stone threshold of a doorway. His hair was sandy brown, his features long and thin. A familiar wet glint in his eyes sparkled in the evening's thick sunlight.

He was dressed formally in top hat and tails. A walking stick—brass monkey's head for a handle—was held lightly in one hand. Before him a sidewalk moved by, carrying with it men and women dressed in a similar style: men in top hats and tails, women in evening gowns accessorized with scarves of some modern miracle fiber that trailed weightlessly behind them in pastel clouds. In the streets, brightly colored plastic cars glided by silently, powered by some clean and efficient energy of the future.

Yellow light glinted off the sidewalk railing, the traffic, the brass, gold and silver heads of many walking sticks, the tall buildings and the long glass tubes that connected one to another. Overhead a dark dirigible moved slowly through the blue sky.

The young man traveled several blocks on the moving sidewalk, nodding occasionally at a friendly or familiar face that passed by in the opposite direction. He glanced up at the sky, the sun, and the dirigible, then down at the silver pocket watch he pulled from a vest pocket.

A beautiful young woman in a sea-foam gown smiled at him from the opposite sidewalk. He was taken by surprise, and a stunned, slightly stupid expression fixed itself onto his face. There was some special radiance in her smile, some quality of open affection or attraction; the young man craned his neck to look back after she passed, but she was already lost in a crowd of tuxedos, top hats, and taffeta. The glittering city slid smoothly by.

The buildings became smaller, less frequent and less shiny. The man transferred from the moving sidewalk to immovable concrete with a small, hopping step. He stopped before a white house. He walked up a bright path leading to a porch framed by white pillars and red flowers. A wooden swing hung from two thin chains. The man paused outside the front door to gaze at the porch swing. He seemed to be studying it, perhaps recalling some moment of his youth that was spent there or in a place like it. Did he smile wistfully or ruefully?

The swing moved gently in an unseen breeze.

He knocked on the door and after a moment it opened. It was Susan—his mother, my sister. She had aged, but gracefully. Her hair was frosted lightly at the sides and front, and the pencil thin marks around her eyes and mouth were like the unconvincing grease paint lines drawn onto the face of an actor to indicate the passage of time. She smiled at her son at the door and the lines deepened.

"Hello Mother," Robert said.

"Robert," his mother said with open arms. He hugged her awkwardly, gazing absently over her shoulder.

"Is anyone else here yet?"

"Just your Uncle Thomas."

Inside a friendly, cluttered living room, Thomas rose from the couch to greet his nephew. They shook hands, nodded, and exchanged the usual greetings. Thomas was completely bald, wearing thick glasses, and stood a little stooped at the shoulders. He was thin the way certain old men are thin, with cords rising from the crepe flesh of their necks and brittle bones pressing out sharply against skin and fabric.

"How have you been, Robert?" he asked in a voice that was deeper and thinner than the one I had known. "Working you hard at the company?"

"They get their money out of me," Robert said.

"I bet they do," said Thomas. "They get their due." He chuckled quietly to himself.

A dog, old and blocky, came waddling into the room on bowed legs. Robert stooped to scratch its black and silver head and let it sniff at his presumably familiar hand.

"How are you, Mac?" he said. It was not a dog I had ever seen before, but already it was aged and well-known to the people in the room. Its years as a mischievous puppy, a restless adolescent, a frustrated adult, had all been lost to me. It had gone from the incontinence of infancy to the incontinence of the aged without me.

How much had taken place in this world while I was not watching, while I had worked and wooed and did not win? It frightened me. I had lost the thread of these lives that had once meant so much to me. Things had continued without me, plots had raveled and unraveled, characters entered and exited, scenes changed, sets torn down and rebuilt. I would never catch up now.

The dog let out a feeble bark. Someone else was at the door.

William and Maggie entered, accompanied by a young girl of sixteen or so. William had grown thick with age and success. His hair was gray and combed thinly across the top of his head, his scalp showing through like the ground beneath the parse grass of winter. Maggie, for her part, had silver hair shaped like a helmet. There were puckered lines around her mouth—the kind you see in women who have made a certain face, or who smoked or spoke French for too long.

The girl, who I quickly quessed was their daughter, combined what was once attractive in them both, adding to that the wet gloss of youth. Her hair was long and golden, her mouth full and red, her eyes large and having a particular shade of blue that gave the impression of virginal innocence.

There was much handshaking, hugs, friendly greetings, kissing of cheeks. The old dog moved slowly from one guest to another, sniffing the cuffs of pants, nuzzling a bare shin, and then, satisfied that he knew all and that all belonged, he collapsed into a corner of the room to pant and drool upon his graying paws.

Suddenly, the blank space of one wall became alive with explosions, a man running in slow motion from out of a blossoming fireball, and the scream of a child.

"Daddy!" the child's voice said. "Daddy, help me!"

All in the room turned absently to watch these events noisily unfolding between the kitchen doorway and a china cabinet.

"What's this?" William asked. "I know this."

"Yes," Thomas said. "It's that thing . . . you know . . . with the one guy."

"Which guy?"

"The guy who was in the other thing."

"This is old," the girl said to Robert in the conspiratorial aside of youth in a room full of age.

"I think I've seen it," Robert said. "Is it the one with the mad bomber?" he asked his uncles.

"Yes," said Thomas. "The mad bomber with one arm. The hero cuts it off . . ."

"And beats him with it?" William offered, pursing his lips and trying to remember.

"It *is* old," Robert said to the young girl.

"You're thinking of the other one," Maggie told her husband.

"I don't think he beats him with it," Thomas said.

"It looks old," the young girl said.

A quiet fell upon the room as the five of them stood watching for a moment. The hero of the scene was running across a metal scaffold in what appeared to be an abandoned factory. He stopped cold as he saw the mad bomber standing at the opposite end, holding a sobbing little yellow-haired girl in front of him by the neck.

"Leave her alone, Kranavich," the hero said.

"It's me you want."

"You're wrong, Bremmer," he hissed, as he held up a stiff, black, lifeless hand. "It's my hand I want. And you can't get that back for me, can you?"

"I thought it was his whole arm he was missing," William said. "How the heck can you beat a guy with just a severed hand?"

Robert and the girl laughed, and Maggie shook her head.

"You're thinking of the other one," Thomas said.

Susan entered the room.

"Turn it off," she said. "Dinner's ready."

The TV became a blank space on the wall again. They filed out and entered the dining room.

A table was set with white tablecloth, flower-patterned china, silverware, wineglasses. I wondered what the occasion was, and why Robert's father was not there. Was it Robert's 32nd or 33rd (or 34th) birthday? Was it Christmas or Easter? Had his father left or died?

It was Thanksgiving, I slowly came to realize, and his father had died some years before. I could sense it by the arrangement of dried flowers at the center of the table and the empty chair at the head that went unnoticed. There were photos on a mantle with faces squinting into a long-past sun. A large roasted turkey was served and wine was poured into the glasses.

"Should someone say grace?" Susan asked when everyone had their well-balanced arrangement of red, white, green and brown on the plates in front of them.

"Do we ever say grace?" Robert asked.

"I don't recall anyone doing it last year," William said, but Thomas stood up, raising a glass.

"I would like to say something, if I may," he said.

Eyes turned toward him. Glasses were raised, and all waited for Thomas to continue.

"This is a day for giving thanks," Thomas said. "But it's also a day for remembering a bit, I think." He paused, and seemed to start over from another place.

"We are gathered here together today because we are family. But I would like to say something about the members of our family who are not here with us today. My mother and father . . ."

William looked down at the table, and his eyes fell to his plate of food with an unseeing look.

"Your father, Robert, who was like a brother to me and William."

Robert, smiling gently, nodded at his uncle.

"And my brother James," he said.

"Our brother," William added.

Thomas corrected himself: "Our brother

James." He raised his glass higher, signifying the end of his toast. "To all who have gone before us. We still remember and love you. And give thanks."

Glasses clinked together and sips of wine were taken. One word from the toast—the summary of all its words—was muttered back and forth with each little chime of glass hitting glass. "Thanks," they all said.

I turned off the TV and cried. No, it was not crying, but weeping, intense weeping, the sort of tears that seem wrung from the wetness of the brain itself, leaving behind a strange and clean emptiness when it is done.

I finished weeping and went for a walk.

A gentle, warm rain was falling from a lead-colored sky. I walked to the liquor store and got a bottle.

I took burning sips of it as I walked back home, the bottle wrapped in a now- damp brown paper bag bunched by my fist around the bottle's neck. I had seen derelicts in both my lives and this was how they walked the streets. A bag shaped like a bottle in their fist. Half a block and then pause for a sip. Wipe mouth with back of hand. Squint out at the world as if at any moment it might change.

The streets were empty; there were only the distant barks of dying cars and the soft hiss of rain.

Back inside, I made wet squeaking steps up

the stairs to her door. I knocked. She answered, wearing clothes for the first time since I had known her: a spring dress, short, black with tiny white flowers. It was made of some airy material that lifted at the slightest breeze and almost let through the light. It was held up by thin straps over her round pale shoulders. The back was scooped low enough to allow her wings an exit.

"Hello," I said to her. "It's Thanksgiving. Come with me and we will give thanks."

"How can you tell?" she said with the smallest, gentlest laugh.

I pounded my fist dramatically against my chest. "I can feel it here!"

"I'll get my shoes then. If you can feel it there. I'll get my shoes."

She put on sandals and we were off, walking through puddles and mist, taking turns at the bottle.

"Thanks! I am giving thanks!" she said and laughed every time I handed her the wet, bottle-shaped bag. Then the bottle slipped through the wet paper and broke against the sidewalk. We jumped back, startled. Her hand flew to her mouth in surprise, taking two small white knuckles between her teeth.

"Alas, Old Faithful," I said. "We hardly knew ye."

The glass on the pavement glistened and jittered like distant stars. The lead sky became charcoal and then velvet. We spent hours (days? weeks?) stumbling through the dead streets. A night that lasted forever, laughing drunk and sad, her wet feathers grazing against my cheek. I held her close to me at a corner and kissed her.

"So what is your name?" I whispered into her ear.

"It's Angel!"

"No . . ."

"Angelica?" she offered. "Angela?"

"A rose by any other name," I muttered with my lips blurring the words against her face.

"My name is Rose," she laughed.

We arrived back at our building, walked through the always-open red door, across the threadbare rug, past the worn leather couch. The still life hung crooked on the wall.

"Would you like to see my place?" I asked her.

"Of course," she said, leaning against me as we walked up the stairs.

I showed her my place, but it seemed strangely barren now, as if I had been robbed of things I had forgotten I owned. The TV, the couch, and the night-light by the bed were all still there, but something was missing. I turned on the night-light. We lay down on my small bed, and with one arm holding her close I pointed an unsteady finger at the light slipping across the walls and ceiling of my room.

"It's like magic," she said.

"Isn't it though?"

"It is."

"It is," I agreed. "My mother used to put it on for me to sleep to. Dear old mother . . ."

"Let us give thanks . . ."

"Look," I said as the watery light glided over the crack in the ceiling. "What does that look like to you?"

"Is that where I hit my head dancing? It looks like a battle. A great war between fish and squirrels. Right now the fish are winning but the squirrel king is entering the fray, coming over the hill on a great horse. He's holding a long spear. He has a fierce look on his face and some of his soldiers are looking up at him as he approaches. They're hopeful now. Though some of them are just dead of course."

I thought about it, studied it, but could not make the lines form any of this.

"Does it?" I asked.

"A little."

I let my hand fall upon the smooth skin of her leg. I let it slide up unresisted, pushing aside the light fabric of her dress. I let it travel the unbroken line of her flesh, over her hip, across soft white belly and soft white breast, until I touched the hardening point at its tip. I felt the alien folds and dampness between her legs and kissed the fluttering lids of her eyes, the bridge of her nose, her mouth. In her mouth, and in my drunkenness, I could almost forget everything. A seamless kiss that led seamlessly to still other things, with the childhood light of Niagara Falls moving over everything. The nostalgic smell of burnt dust in the air was not a distraction, nor the soft, falling rain through leaves, nor the creak of bedsprings.

But the unity of two becoming one is a thing—a dream—that never quite lives up to its advertising. The transcendent moment, if it occurs, is fleeting, and dissolves quickly back into the inescapable and common scene of two soft human shells bouncing. It cannot last, for both physical and spiritual reasons, and whatever it is that might briefly verge on vision, wordless poetry, tuneless music, etc., soon becomes again only a matter of positions, endurance, cramping muscles, sweat, and the inevitable finish. Two do not become one. One becomes everything and reaches its logical conclusion of exclamation, deflation, and exhaustion. Eventually we tire and we sleep. But now I no longer dreamed.

# CLOUD 8

Morning came without a golden shaft of sunlight, but only the lead-gray sky becoming pale, with no part of it brighter than the rest, as if there were no sun at all, but only the soft glow of the sky itself.

I was alone in my bed. I got up, walked naked through my apartment, and still felt that something was missing. Besides the angel, I mean. She was gone, but that was expected. It was some other thing that was lacking. I cleaned the dishes in the sink. I banged a small chip from the rim of my Daffy Duck glass with the heavy handle of a knife, but did not shed a tear.

For a second, I thought I heard the angel's footsteps above me. They grew lighter, as if her wings finally worked and were lifting her slowly from the floor. I pictured her flying out the window, a crooked line through the sky until she was swallowed by the gray, featureless sheet of clouds.

I got dressed and went to work.

# -34-

The building had once seemed so tall, shiny and undamaged. Now I saw the smudges and streaks on its glass front, the wear and scuff marks along its marble floors, the frayed cuff of the security guard's uniform and the threadbare, soiled carpet of the elevator.

My desk had waited patiently for me, but as I entered the vast wall-less area of my department, it seemed as if a dust of strangeness had fallen over everything.

Mary was where she should have been. She smiled warmly at me, a look of pleasant surprise glittering in her eyes. I nodded and smiled back. I scanned the room and saw everyone in their place, though there may have been less *everyone* now than there had been before. The anonymous faces, the temp secretaries, the people I never got to know seemed to have gracefully left, taking the spaces they occupied with them. Marge Boyton, John Landsdale, and Steven Roth were still there, all doing their designated jobs in their assigned seats. I sat down in my seat and turned on the computer. I stared at it. I stared outside at the highest building, the slab of sky teetering on its point. Then I turned off the computer, stood up, and walked slowly across the floor toward John Landsdale's desk.

"It's all done," I said to the manager. He looked up with his pale, bloodless face and waterless eyes.

"Is it?"

"Yes."

"Well, thank you then."

His eyes fell back to his own computer and his fingers clicked expertly across the keyboard. I turned, walked away, and, passing Mary on my way out, brushed my hand across her shoulder by way of goodbye.

I walked to the post office. There was an envelope waiting for me. Inside the envelope was an address. I took it back outside where a taxi was waiting, a white cab with rust bleeding down from the door handles and crusting around the wheel wells. I got in and handed the address to the Abraham Lincoln behind the wheel. He nodded, the car lurched forward, and the back bumper was left behind us in the road.

"Is it far?" I asked him.

"Are you in a hurry?" he asked me.

"No," I said. "Just curious."

Pieces of the car fell behind us. A rusty trail of bread crumbs. He slammed on the brakes at an intersection to avoid a bus and my head jerked forward, banging against the glass that separated me and the driver. I had not even realized the glass was there. I reached up to touch the spot where my head hit and there was blood on my fingertips.

"You OK?" the driver asked.

"Sure," I said.

But the window between us is cracked now. As he drives on, hitting chuckholes and rough seams of pavement, the crack spreads out across the glass, until bits of it are falling down onto the floor at my feet. The driver is unconcerned and I decide to be unconcerned as well. Even when large shards of it topple down like pieces of a glacier. Even when the side door falls off and spins to a stop in the road behind us.

I lean forward to the now open space between us and say: "Your car is falling apart." He nods. Even as the front windshield dissolves into a spray of glass beads. Even as the panels of the car drop away one by one with no more weight or resistance than playing cards. Even as the road and countryside blowing by grow dark and the seat I was sitting on disappears into its own shadows and the driver himself is gone. Now everything is only a dark tunnel. A long black tunnel with a bright light at the end of it. A tall thin figure stands in the light. What waits for me up ahead? Is it a purer and brighter light? A better job in a taller building with truer love and satisfaction than I have ever known before? Maybe it is the heaven I once knew with the certainty of youth—a heaven of winged angels (more than one), golden trumpets, white clouds, divine museums and a choir of sweet voices. Perhaps the tall thin figure is the ghost of the real Abraham Lincoln greeting me, beckoning me onward to a place of true happiness and fulfillment. I am closer now. It is my father. Closer still. It is my mother.

I will ask for cardboard wings.